FIGHTING HER *Touch*

BOOK 2

HEALING HEARTS
A *Lesbian Medical Romance* Drama Series

MT CASSEN

A dedication from Morgan Cassen to medical workers in all corners of our world:

Morgan is in awe of the work done by the frontline workers of the noblest profession. The recent events have only increased my appreciation of the difficulty and danger associated with your line of work. I would like to thank you from the bottom of my heart.

CHAPTER ONE

T he breakroom smelled of burnt popcorn as Elizabeth Fletcher stepped inside. She chewed her lower lip, the weight of the world pressing on her shoulders. A few people were sprinkled throughout the breakroom. One woman sat along the windowsill, her phone in hand as she looked up and nodded her greeting. Liz gave a slight wave, but the woman had already looked back down. A man sat in the corner, eating something that looked like cereal, or perhaps oatmeal, his eyes locked on a woman who was halfway across the room. She seemed oblivious to his gaze, or maybe she was playing it cool.

Liz quickly looked away. The last thing she wanted was for him to catch her staring, and she was probably too tired for decent conversation. Her eyes darted to the microwave as another woman who looked to be in her mid- to late forties took the popcorn out of the microwave and opened it up, dumping the contents into a bowl. Her eyes caught Liz's, and she grinned.

"Breakfast of champions, right here," she said. "Want some?"

Liz smiled and held up a granola bar. "Thanks, though." She walked over to an empty chair and collapsed into it, careful not to make too much of a disruption as she tore back the wrapper. Liz released a sigh and took a small bite out of the bar.

Three weeks into the job at Capmed, and still, she wasn't all that comfortable. She kept her eyes drawn to the top of the table, hoping that if she did happen to look up, no one would be staring. Just fifteen minutes; she could handle fifteen minutes of waiting out clock-in time. She was already positive that the day would be a busy one. That was one thing about her nursing gig; she never had to worry about downtime. If she wasn't rushing around trying to learn the ropes from a fellow nurse, she was being pulled in a thousand different directions to help out where needed. Every day, she returned home with aching feet, an aching back, and a throbbing headache. What if she wasn't cut out to be a nurse?

Give this shot. Transport this patient here. Don't do that. No, do that. File these records. She was exhausted just thinking about it.

In all honesty, she was glad she chose to go to nursing school, but she somehow thought this path would have more flexibility. *Give yourself time, Liz. Geesh. You're less than a month in.* She was a little naive but liked to call it optimism.

"This seat taken?"

She looked up. The woman with the burnt popcorn stood propped against her chair. Liz shook her head, scared even to fathom turning the woman away. She looked like she could throttle a person if they even dared to disagree with her.

"Thanks!" The woman slid down onto the chair and popped a handful of popcorn into her mouth. "I'm exhausted."

Liz frowned. "The day hasn't even started."

The woman laughed. "For you, maybe. For me, though, I've been here ten hours and eleven minutes." She glanced at her watch. "Correction! Twelve minutes."

She released a yawn before she scarfed down some more popcorn. "Last night, the ER was swamped. I saw ten patients the first hour." She released another yawn. "Don't worry, though. Took care of them all before you got here." She smirked and turned back to her popcorn.

Liz nodded politely and looked away. Her gaze returned to the woman on the windowsill. She was wearing a lab coat, so she was probably a doctor. Something about her was alluring. She looked older than Liz and pretty, but it was something else drawing Liz in. The way she carried herself. And her eyes…

After a moment, the woman glanced up, and Liz quickly looked away, her cheeks warming. Why had she been staring? Must have been the exhaustion. Liz shoved the last of her granola bar into her mouth.

"You're new around here, right?"

Liz turned her attention back to the woman sitting across from her. "Newish," Liz stuttered, then coughed, her granola bar going down the wrong pipe.

The woman jumped up and went around to pound on Liz's back. "Are you okay?" she asked.

Liz coughed, attempting to catch her breath, then held up

her hand. "I'm fine," she exclaimed, clearing her throat, and looked up at the woman. "Yeah, I'm good. Thanks."

She coughed again to clear her throat, then nodded. "As I was saying—new, as in I've been here three weeks. Pulmonology floor."

"Snoozefest!" the woman said, making a fake yawn, then smirked. "Just teasing. Someone's got to do it, right?" She then quirked up an eyebrow. "Silly me, I sometimes get off on these tangents. I haven't even introduced myself. Name's Hanna."

She stuck out her hand for Liz to shake. Hanna had this infectious smile that made Liz want to respond in kind. "I've been here going on twenty-one years. So, you being here three weeks, that's definitely new." She laughed loudly, which brought a smirk to Liz's lips.

Twenty-one years *was* a long time, considering Liz was only twenty-three. "Elizabeth!" she responded, then looked down at her name badge. She wanted to crawl under the table and hide. "Obviously."

Hanna giggled, then held up her badge, which hung down at her waist. "Don't want people to find my name easily." She winked.

"You'll find there isn't a very rapid turnover here. Hey, Rob," she called out to the man who was checking out a nurse several tables away. He quickly glanced over and arched an eyebrow. "How long have you worked here?"

"Too long," he muttered.

Hanna tilted her head. "Serious answers only, please."

"Who said I wasn't serious?" He then smirked and slid his eyes to Liz's. "Ten years."

"See," Hanna replied. "He started when he was ten."

Rob rolled his eyes, but the woman he had been eyeing laughed, which made Rob grin and turn back to her. "That was pretty funny, huh?" he asked, a sly smirk attached to his lips.

Hanna shook her head. "Let's just call him the hospital flirt."

"I have a boyfriend," Liz quickly pointed out.

Hanna tossed her head back and howled. "I'll tell ya, honey. That has never stopped him before."

Hanna turned to the woman who was now engrossed in a conversation with Rob. "That's Sally. She's been here over twelve years, so once you're here, you're here for life. She works in the ER part-time and the cardiology department the rest of her time." She tossed a look to Liz. "And in case you were wondering, yes, Sally is fully aware that Rob is crushing on her. Which is fine, because frankly," she held her hand up to her mouth, so no one else could hear her, "she feels the same."

Liz smiled. In those fifteen minutes, she had suddenly gotten the whole landscape of the hospital with one quick swoop. Already three weeks in and this was the first time she felt comfortable.

She couldn't help but glance back at the woman on the windowsill. "Who is that?" she asked Hanna.

Hanna turned her head to look. "Oh, that's Marisa. But be careful with her. She can be a bit—"

Liz shot to her feet, just noticing the time. "Shoot! Sorry. I have to clock in, but it was nice meeting you."

"Same to you, Liz. Sure I'll see ya around." She waved and went back to her popcorn. Liz couldn't hide her smile as she tossed away her wrapper and clocked in for her shift, for once expecting that her day would run just as smoothly.

To Liz's dismay, while the moments before her shift were the best fifteen minutes of her three weeks at the hospital, things slowly derailed from there.

"Are you a nurse?" a woman asked, rushing up to her just five minutes after she clocked in.

"Um, yeah, I mean yes…" Liz held out her badge, which she had moved to her waist. She turned from the elevator, which was only seconds away from opening. "Do you need something?"

Sure, it was a hospital, and everyone needed help of some kind, but Liz wasn't supposed to nab patients out of the waiting room. Some protocols needed to be followed, and Liz had been reminded of that repeatedly throughout training.

"My kid," the woman said. "She has a nasty bump. She fell. I need someone to take a look at her."

"Did you sign her in?" Liz asked, looking over at the front desk where three other people were waiting to be checked in. This wasn't even her floor. She was headed two floors up. She turned back to the woman. "If you have her signed in, then they'll—"

"They'll be with her. I've heard that story, ma'am. But we've been waiting for thirty minutes now, and she's not looking well."

Liz sighed and forced a smile. "Have a seat, and I'll see what I can find out."

The woman groaned but walked over to where her daughter was. Her daughter was slumped forward, her hands hanging limply. Liz frowned. She was right. The girl didn't look great.

She walked behind the counter where a disheveled-looking

woman was plowing away on her keyboard. Her fingers were angrily typing, her eyes focused on what she was doing.

"Excuse me," Liz whispered. When the woman didn't even acknowledge her, Liz cleared her throat. "I hate to interrupt," she said louder and more forcefully.

The woman cast a glance toward Liz. "Yeah?"

"Could you tell me when you think the woman and her daughter over there will be helped?" Liz fidgeted from one foot to the other, ready for the woman to blast her.

The woman opened her mouth, then snapped her mouth shut before opening it again. "What's her name?"

Liz nervously bit at her lower lip. That would have been a helpful question to ask. At the moment, she hadn't even considered asking something so simple as *What's your name?* before putting herself out there like that.

The front desk clerk rolled her eyes over the intake clipboards. "Have at it." She then turned back to her computer and continued typing before calling the next woman forward.

Liz heaved a sigh and glanced at her watch. She was already fifteen minutes late getting up to her floor, and she could imagine the indecent words she would be spewed out by for not getting to her shift on time.

She rifled through the stack of charts. *Nosebleed, no. Dog bite, no. Car accident, no. No. No. No.* Finally, she pulled out a chart that was for a fall. And the girl's age was thirteen. This had to be it, but it was way at the bottom of the line.

"So, do they go in order?" Liz asked, turning to the woman's back.

"No. not in strict order. The triage nurse evaluates them and ranks the patients in terms of how serious their condition is. The order patients are seen in is the triage nurse's prerogative."

"I see," Liz said.

The woman released a breath, then nodded. "Patients always get impatient in the emergency room. It's par for the course." She swiveled back to face her computer.

Liz reluctantly went back to the woman and her daughter.

"They just have a few more patients to go, and they'll be right with her." Yes, it was a lie, but she didn't know what else to say. She wanted to avoid any further confrontation.

"A few more patients?" the woman asked. "Look around. This waiting room is full of patients. Who says they're more urgent than my daughter?"

"Mom? I feel like I'm going to get sick," the girl said, reaching out for her mother's hand.

Liz felt helpless as she looked around Capmed. She spotted Hanna and hurried over to her as the latter began to grab a chart from the top of the pile.

"Hanna, wait!" Liz hissed, reaching for her hand.

"What are you doing here? You're on the wrong floor, aren't you?"

Liz didn't have time to explain the whole situation as she looked at the woman. "Right place, right time. Or wrong place, wrong time," Liz groaned. "I don't know, but I need your help."

"I'm a little busy right now," Hanna laughed. "I get off in less than two hours. Hit me up then."

"You don't understand," Liz spoke, her voice pleading for Hanna's attention. "That woman and her daughter over there. The daughter is about to get sick, and she's had a nasty fall, and she needs to be seen."

"You're new here," Hanna stated. "The ER is a tough place to be. It's always overflowing beyond capacity. The waiting room may look busy, but it's a lot busier back there." She motioned to the hall where the doctors were working. Liz looked over to the girl, who lay against her mom's shoulder, her face flushed, then turned back to Hanna.

"Isn't there something that can be done? Maybe give her a bucket that she can throw up in or something. She doesn't look well."

Hanna scrunched up her nose and looked over to her, then glanced back at Liz. "Let me check on her."

Liz smiled and looked over at the woman and her daughter, then back to Hanna. "Thank you!"

From the corner of her eye, she saw the woman at the front desk shake her head, her face etched like stone.

Liz stepped back from the desk and hurried to the elevator. As the doors closed her in, she fell back against the wall and tried to control her breathing. Liz could already imagine the repercussions that would come from doing something that others would surely feel was quite trivial.

When the elevator doors opened, three people turned to gawk at her. "We were wondering where you were," Vicky, the lead nurse, said. "I hope you have a good answer."

Liz wasn't confident that anything she could say would get her out of this mess. Especially when she had already disobeyed their biggest rule: Follow protocol or expect to be reprimanded. She just hoped that it wouldn't be at the expense of her job.

CHAPTER TWO

Marisa

The hallway was empty. Employees were stashed in rooms working on patients or patients were all stuck in the waiting room waiting to be seen. Marisa pushed through the breakroom door, expecting it to also be empty. It was halfway between lunch and supper. Typically, that meant her break gave her time to reflect on her day instead of being forced to talk to someone when she would rather...not. *Lab Weekly*, a blog published every Monday, was already calling out her name. Instead, she entered the room to find a woman trying to demolish the vending machine.

Marisa smiled. It was the same woman she had seen earlier in the breakroom near the start of the day. The one who had looked away from her bashfully. Marisa's gaze trailed down the young woman's body. Her scrubs were loose, but they didn't hide the woman's nice figure.

"Come on, you stupid thing, just give it to me." The woman slammed her fists against the machine, a look of distress coursing all over the lines of her cheekbones. Marisa checked the name on the woman's badge. *Elizabeth.*

"What'd that machine ever do to you?" Marisa asked just as Elizabeth forced her elbow into the machine. She looked at Marisa, her eyes wide, before collecting herself.

"For starters, not giving me my chocolate. Which I desperately need." She punched her fist against the spot that held her chocolate bar in place, then groaned. "Looks like maybe I'm just not supposed to have it. The universe has a funny sense of humor."

She pushed on the coin return. "And I guess I'm not supposed to get my money back, either. Go figure. About covers my day," she grumbled, dropping into the nearest chair.

Marisa walked over and punched the side of her fist into the machine. Immediately, the bar was released. She reached down to grab it, then tossed it over to Elizabeth's table.

Elizabeth grabbed the bar and stared at it before releasing a soft laugh. Marisa's heart skipped a few beats. That laugh was much better than the anger on her face a few moments ago. And her smile was stunning. But why so much frustration over a chocolate bar? She was sure there was more to it than that.

"Thanks," Elizabeth grumbled.

Marisa shrugged. "It's all in the wrist. I've had to release plenty in my day." She turned back to the vending machine, considering its plethora of options, then slipped her money back into her pocket and went to an empty table. "First day?" she asked, sitting down and crossing her legs, propping them up in a chair.

Elizabeth chomped down on the bar and turned to look at her. She snickered and shook her head, taking another bite into her mouth. "Might be easier if it were." She pulled out her phone and started scrolling.

Marisa did the same, figuring the woman might need some time alone. She pulled up *Lab Weekly* and skimmed through it to find her article.

Might be easier if it were. Those words played on a continuous loop through Marisa's mind. She finally looked up, ignoring the article. "Long day?"

"Might be my last day," Elizabeth mumbled, setting her phone down and pulling a crumpled-up paper from her pocket. After tossing it on the table, she rested her head in her hands.

Marisa got up from her chair and went over to pick it up, despite barely knowing this woman. She had a weakness for beautiful women and this one also intrigued her. "Dear Elizabeth Fletcher," she started, "please report to conference room B tomorrow before your shift. We have some things to discuss with you and expect your prompt arrival."

She laughed, tossing the paper back onto the center of the table. "I wouldn't worry too much about it. We've all received letters similar to this in our employment."

Elizabeth looked up at her. Her eyes were narrowed into a thin line, her eyebrow was quirked up, and her lips were curved into a frown. Marisa lingered on those full lips for a moment too long. They were soft pink and looked completely natural, just how Marisa preferred.

Marisa shrugged. "I'm telling you. This letter alone doesn't scream termination. Take it from someone who's been around."

Without being asked, she took the seat across from Elizabeth. "Besides, they're having you finish out your day, right? That alone is promising. Also, they said, and I quote, 'before your shift.'" Its meaning seemed obvious to her, but Elizabeth's eyes continued to darken. "Why would they put that phrasing if they were planning on terminating you? It's spelled out right there. Don't you think?"

"I don't know." Elizabeth grabbed the letter, reading over it intently. Marisa knew it was most likely the thousandth time Elizabeth was reading those words. Why force herself to read them again?

"You're at an unfair disadvantage," Marisa stated. "I know your name, but you don't know mine. Marisa Cavanaugh. I'm the laboratory manager." She forced her hand out to Elizabeth. "It's a shame we're meeting when you're looking so upset."

She quirked her lips into a smile, but Elizabeth didn't respond. "I don't know you, Elizabeth, but I'd say you might be a worrier. Maybe just a little bit?" A worrier—or slightly immature. After all, she did look to be much younger than Marisa.

Elizabeth set the letter down, her expression even more tense. "I guess I've been told I am. But I've never been fired a day in my life. I was hoping that wouldn't change when I started this nursing venture."

Marisa raised her brows, making her smile wider. "Then have faith because you don't know why they're calling you to the conference room. I really wouldn't worry about it. Not to mention, what could you have possibly done that you think deems termination?"

Elizabeth sighed as Marisa waited for the explanation. Elizabeth proceeded to tell her the story of how an incident in the emergency room had led to her being late for her shift. Marisa simply listened, no longer interested in the article that was still on her phone. When Elizabeth was done, she seemed less tense.

Marisa nodded. "I can see you're still worried about it," she started. "The good news is, though, your eyes have softened considerably since I entered the room."

Elizabeth laughed, her cheeks turning into a rosy hue. *That's better.* Marisa nodded, forcing herself not to stare at Elizabeth's lips and imagine what they might taste like. She wanted to see Elizabeth smile, not fret over something she had no control over. That wasn't going to help anyone, least of all Elizabeth.

"I think you're worrying over nothing. Everything you just told me doesn't sound like something they would fire someone over. How long have you worked here?"

"Three weeks." Elizabeth covered her face and shook her head. "If I'm fired after three weeks, I'll never be able to live that down." She dropped her hands and turned her gaze to Marisa. She clearly cared what others thought about her, but it wasn't good to hold that much anxiety over what anyone else might think.

"Just try to relax and enjoy the rest of the day. By this time tomorrow, you'll probably be laughing about the fact that you were so worried."

Those words brought a bigger smile to Elizabeth's face, which Marisa enjoyed seeing, but deep down, Marisa had some worries about the matter. Capmed was usually an easy place to work unless the higher-ups felt compelled to make an example of someone. Marisa just hoped she wasn't giving Elizabeth some false sense of security. Or else she was liable to push the woman deeper into the emotional hole she seemed to be in.

Even more worrisome was Marisa's strong attraction to this woman. Their age gap was too big to pursue anything, so hopefully they wouldn't see much of each other. She didn't need any relationship drama right now.

Still, Elizabeth was cute.

After finishing her candy bar, Elizabeth stood and dusted her hands. "Well, I should get back. It was nice meeting you."

"You, too."

Elizabeth paused a moment, then bit her lower lip and turned back to Marisa. "You can call me Liz."

Marisa nodded, fighting the butterflies in her stomach. Was she imagining it, or was Liz being a little flirty? "Bye, Liz," she said, waving, as Liz scurried out of the breakroom.

This isn't going to end well.

MARISA STEPPED OUTSIDE TO THE WAITING BREEZE AND TOOK IN a deep breath. Freedom. She always loved the smell of that. While Marisa loved her job as a laboratory manager, she sometimes felt like the world was passing her by. Maybe that was because there were times when Marisa had to stand back and wonder if she had rushed into things in life.

Marisa's life hadn't always panned out the way she had intended. After high school, she had anticipated seeing the world, maybe going to France, Italy, the Virgin Islands, or a million other places to explore. But life quickly derailed when her parents were killed in a house fire while she was away visiting her grandparents.

She realized then that life had a way of changing you. Marisa needed a way to take care of herself and threw herself into her studies. She graduated with honors and did her internship at the hospital. Right away, she was hired and never looked back. Now, at the age of forty-two, she wondered if there was more to life than hard work.

"Marisa! Wait up!"

She turned on her heel just before reaching the parking lot. Samantha came running up to her. "Thought that was you. You were on a mission to get out of here."

Marisa snickered. "Don't you ever feel that way?"

Samantha shrugged. "Remember, when I go home, I'm going home to a house full of people. My grandmother, mom, dad, pregnant sister, and her two-year-old. So, no, not really." She laughed and looked around the front of the hospital before turning her gaze back to Marisa. "I'm probably delaying you from getting on home. To your empty house and all."

Samantha tilted her head. "Don't you ever feel it's lonely?"

Marisa scrunched up her nose in thought, then shrugged. "Maybe, but honestly, when you just said how hectic your house is, it wore me out." Marisa smiled, which made Samantha laugh.

"Besides, tonight will not be one of those lonely nights." She laughed. "I have a bottle of wine calling out my name and a night of Netflix on my agenda."

Marisa stared at Samantha, wondering if there was a real reason she had stopped her. They were friends, or at least friendly, at the hospital, and had only hung out a few times outside of work. Samantha was twenty-one, and all their similar-ities ended with working in the same department.

Samantha worked at the front desk of the lab. She had started at the age of eighteen, right out of high school, and seemed more mature than most people who had held the job. Marisa supposed she had to grow up pretty fast after seeing her older sister managing a baby as a single parent, with another one on the way.

They walked together out of the hospital and into the parking lot. Samantha lingered by Marisa's side, a little too close. "Hey, I was thinking—"

"Hi," a familiar voice said; Marisa turned to see who it was. Her heart fluttered when she saw Liz approaching.

Marisa waved. "Remember what I said, Liz. I'm sure tomorrow you'll see you were worrying for nothing."

Liz smiled, the widest Marisa had seen since their encounter earlier in the day. "Thank you! Your pep talk helped. I do feel a little better. Well, I have to go, but have a good night." She waved and hurried off to the parking lot.

Liz's ponytail swished in the wind as she jogged toward her car. She was on a mission to get out of there as well.

Samantha cleared her throat, making Marisa turn back to her. Samantha's mood had grown stormy and her words were clipped. "Who was that woman?"

It was a quick change of subject, one that caught Marisa off guard. "Oh, just a nurse who works here. I met her today, and she got a letter from the hospital stating they wanted to meet with her."

"Interesting," Samantha replied. "Getting terminated?"

"She thinks so, but doubtful. I mean, what she's being called in for is so trivial." She started to explain before frowning. "How'd the conversation get to this?" She laughed loudly.

Samantha directed her eyes away from Marisa's, then shrugged. "You looked interested or something."

"I what?" Marisa squealed. "You were reading that all wrong," she argued.

Marisa cast a look over to the parking lot, where her eyes landed on Liz getting into her car. "It's absurd, really. For many reasons. The main one being, what is she, twelve?" She laughed. "No way—no. How am I going to rob that cradle?"

Samantha scrunched up her face. "She's older than me, I'd say."

Marisa laughed. "Well, okay, but we're not talking about you and me in that fashion. We're talking about you thinking you saw something when there's clearly nothing." She quickly shook her head, knowing she was trying to convince herself more than she was Samantha. "Besides, I think the whole hospital knows the toll that Shana took on me. I'm not going to go there again."

"Guess I misread the look, then."

"Glad that's out of the way," Marisa replied. "I should get home."

"Uh, wait," Samantha said. "What if I join you tonight?" She looked away, fidgeting with her bracelet. "Or we can go out. I'm happy to give you some company."

Marisa fished her keys from her purse. "Thanks, but I'll be okay."

"Are you sure?" Samantha grabbed her arm, stepping so close that Marisa could feel the heat radiating off her skin. "I promise I won't argue about what Netflix show we watch. I'll even supply the wine."

Marisa stepped away, pulling free of Samantha's grip. "That's sweet, but I really just want to relax alone tonight. Maybe some other time."

Samantha looked ready to say more but closed her mouth and turned away with a weak nod.

She must really not want to go home tonight. But I'm not up for company. "I'll see you tomorrow," Marisa said.

"Bye," Samantha replied, rushing off.

Marisa felt a little guilty about rejecting Samantha's offer to hang out, but she preferred a quiet evening focused on what she wanted to watch on Netflix and the kind of wine she was rearing to drink.

She reached her car, her mind on Shana and how similar they had been to each other. They both had to work through college in pursuit of their dreams. Sixteen years. That was how many years they had known each other before they decided to try their hand at a relationship.

And for four years, that relationship was good. It was one of the best things Marisa thought she had done in life. Then one day, it was gone. Shana decided her happily ever after wasn't with Marisa, and Marisa was left confused and brokenhearted. Not even a year apart could erase the years they had spent together, and Marisa wasn't really interested in starting up a new relationship. But when she did decide to find someone to be with, she wasn't going to look at someone she had to help mature. She didn't have time for that.

CHAPTER THREE

Liz

Liz looked at her reflection. If she could just crawl back into bed, she knew her aching muscles would be happier. Instead, she was dressed up in a black dress two inches above the knee, a slit that came up the side of her right leg, and heels that matched. She reached across the dresser and grabbed her beaded necklace. Her boyfriend, Chad, had gotten the necklace for her on their first anniversary. Since she was going out with him, it was only fitting that she would wear it. It added to the ensemble, but her heart still crashed hard against her chest.

Liz's thoughts turned to the hospital, and she felt this knot welling up in the pit of her stomach. Her chest tightened, and her head swirled with thoughts of what she was going to say to her supervisor. She couldn't recall the last time she was ever in trouble, but it would have been way back into her elementary school days. Even then, nothing would compare to the angst she would feel in that conference room the following day.

Don't think about it, Liz. Just go out tonight and enjoy yourself.

Way easier said than done. One last look at her reflection, and she was ready to leave her house. On the way to the restaurant, her thoughts played in the back of her mind. Why couldn't they have talked to her right then and there? If she were going to be fired, then at least she would have already known. Instead, she was forced to think about it and wonder how much she would need to plead with them for one more chance. It wasn't going to be an easy night to get through.

Liz turned into the restaurant's parking lot. The lot was already packed, and she had to grab one of the last spots in the back of the lot. It felt like it took her hours to get to the front of the restaurant. But finally, a man opened the door for her, greeting her with a smile.

"Welcome to Enrico's Italian Bistrot."

She forced a smile and nodded. "Thank you." The music played louder as she stepped into the dining area and looked around to find Chad.

"May I help you?" a woman asked, approaching the podium.

"I'm meeting someone here. There's a reservation for Hawthorne."

"Chad?" she asked, looking up.

Liz nodded and then was escorted to the very back of the restaurant. Chad always did like seating areas that were secluded. She wasn't the least bit surprised by his attempt to make them as withdrawn as they could have possibly been.

Chad was already sitting at the table and looked up when she approached. He grinned and then stood to his feet.

"Thank you," she said, glancing at the hostess before she walked away.

Chad grabbed Liz's hand and pulled her to him, brushing his lips along hers. "Good evening," he whispered.

Liz gave a weak smile, withdrawing from the kiss. "Good evening."

He waited for her to take a seat. One thing that could always be said about Chad was that he was a perfect gentleman. He did things by the book, making sure that Liz felt like chivalry wasn't dead. She felt good about that, despite other things that nagged at her inner soul.

"I've taken the liberty to order our appetizer and white wine," he started.

"Oh. Okay. I didn't realize I was late." She glanced at her watch. "I'm sorry."

"You're not; you're right on time. I just wanted to get the evening going. I thought it would be nice to have the order started. I've already checked out the menu, so go ahead and see what you think you're going to have."

He clasped his hands together and waited as Liz looked up at him. She was sometimes annoyed by his eagerness to move everything forward and not take a moment to smell the roses. That was his niche, and to love him was to accept it. She smiled and closed the menu, pushing it away from her.

"I'm ready."

"That's my girl," he said. He looked up and motioned for the waitress to come over and take their order. As they waited, Liz nibbled on her lower lip. She couldn't wait to tell Chad about her impending reprimand. She hoped that he would make her feel better about the matter. After all, he was the CEO of his own company and was responsible for seventy-five employees. If anyone knew how to handle the situation, it would be him.

The waitress came to their table and they both placed their order. Liz waited until she was gone before she glanced at him. "You are not going to believe my day," she began. She just hoped she didn't get all choked up as she was telling him about everything that had happened.

"Can't compare to mine," he replied, groaning. "First of all, Stacy and Matt are having an interoffice affair, despite me saying that it's completely unprofessional, but Vicky caught them, and there was a whole lot of drama. And Curtis is threatening to go to another company if he doesn't get a raise." Chad heaved a sigh. "I shouldn't warrant behavior like that with a raise, but I do hate the thought of him switching to another job. I mean, you know that any one of my competitors probably would snatch him up so that they could have our inside secrets."

As Chad continued—running through the whole lineup of employees, it seemed—Liz took a sip of her wine. In typical fashion, she didn't stop him. She felt it wouldn't do any good if she attempted to interrupt him or interject her thoughts into the matter. She just sipped on her wine and patiently waited for her turn.

When he released an exasperated breath, he shook his head. "Tonight is about us, though. I don't know about you, but I would prefer to keep work out of it. What do you say?" He reached across and grabbed Liz's hand, tracing his fingers over her digits. She frowned. Just when she thought she would get someone to lend an ear, too, he turned her away. She nodded as he wished. There was no point in making a fuss.

Just fifteen minutes later, the waitress brought out their food, and they left the work talk behind them.

Sadly, that also meant giving them very little to talk about as they ate their osso buco. "I talked to Mom this morning," he said.

Liz looked up and nodded. "Oh yeah? How's she doing?"

"Good. No complaints." The conversation died at the end of that.

Liz tapped her foot and stared down at her food. Was that their relationship? Lack of conversation was easily the biggest demise she could see coming between them. She knew finances were something that would break up couples, but they didn't have to worry about that, since Chad owned a multi-million-dollar financial corporation. If anything came between them due to money issues, it would be because Chad felt she didn't need to work.

I can take care of you, Liz. Wedding band or not, you don't have to worry about money.

What he didn't take into consideration was her ambition to be able to support herself. And that would always trump Chad being the overprotective man in her life. As they came to the end of their meal, she looked up to see that Chad had his eyes zoned in on her. She blushed and quickly looked down. Maybe that was one reason she was able to see their relationship as continually blossoming. Chad still did have ways of making her blush. But then, that could also be because of her insecurities when she was around him.

"You're staring," she said, lifting her gaze to his.

He smirked. "Because I just happen to have the most beautiful woman in the restaurant. How could I not stare?"

Liz smiled. It was words like that that seemed to brighten her spirits, and that was one characteristic of Chad's that she loved most. "You have no idea how much I needed to hear that," she started, "especially today. It was such a long, tiring day and—"

"No work, remember?" he cut in. "Baby, I will tell you how beautiful you are forever and ever." He winked at her.

"I appreciate that, but work today..." She stopped there, shaking her head. "I need to talk to you about it. I need some advice."

"Later." He reached for her hand. "Tonight, it's just the two of us at this moment. Dance with me."

Liz was reluctant at first. Every time she began to mention the hospital, he quickly shifted to another subject. If it was an oversight on his part, then that was one thing, but over time, it slowly started to look intentional.

"Just dance with me." His voice softened, and he continued to hold her hand. His eyes brightened, pleading.

She stood to her feet, even though there were moments when she wanted to go back to the table and start all over again. He pulled her into his arms as a slow song played. "They're playing our song," he whispered.

Liz listened to the smooth instrumental that played over the speakers. She didn't know they had a song, and she didn't recognize this one. Yet, she went with it. The song slowly pulled the thoughts of the hospital out of her mind, so it was doing the trick. She had longed for the moment when she could go five minutes without worrying about the following morning.

When the song ended, she looked into his eyes.

"I did need that."

He pulled her close and kissed her.

"Let's go back to the table and have some dessert."

Liz touched her stomach. "I don't think I could possibly eat another thing. I'm stuffed."

"Nonsense," he argued. "You have to have dessert." He flagged down the waitress despite Liz's repeated refusals. She wasn't hungry, and if she even attempted to squeeze dessert in, she was positive it wouldn't go well.

"Chad, I don't think I could," she pleaded. He didn't pay attention and ordered two pieces of chocolate cake. When the waitress left the table, she leaned back in her chair and didn't say another word. If making a scene was her only option, then it was best to avoid it altogether.

When the waitress came back, she placed a piece of cake in front of each of them. "Bon appétit," she said just before leaving.

As Liz picked up her fork and stared at the cake, her stomach did flip-flops. "Dig in," Chad ordered.

Liz forced a smile, then slid her fork into the cake. She had just cut off a chunk and was about to eat it when she spotted something shiny slipped inside of the cake's middle. "What the…" She dug her finger into the cake and pulled out a diamond ring. She stared at it, then turned her attention to him.

Chad was already on his knee in front of her. "Elizabeth Fletcher, when we met five years ago, I thought you were just a woman our parents thought I should get to know. I never imagined that I would fall hopelessly, madly in love with you. Yet, you have become everything to me. As I am kneeling in front of you, with all eyes on us, I know that I will be the luckiest man alive. That is, if you say yes. Liz, will you marry me?"

Liz's jaw dropped, her throat going instantly dry. She quickly took a sip of the bland wine that remained in front of her. "Chad…"

"I love you, Elizabeth Fletcher. Make me the happiest man alive."

Liz looked around the restaurant, and her jaw dropped again when she saw her parents standing less than ten feet away from them. Right beside them was Chad's mother. Right behind her, his sister. They had this all planned down to the very moment she would say yes. How could she say no and disappoint all of them? She did have feelings for Chad, she had just never thought about marriage. But marriage was the next step, right? It would make everyone happy.

Liz turned back to him. "Yes, I'll marry you, Chad."

Her hands shook as he placed the ring on her finger. What else could she possibly have said with all eyes on her? She had to say yes, but the minute that word left her, her stomach clenched. What had she just gotten herself into?

THE DIAMOND THAT SAT ON LIZ'S RING FINGER STILL FELT strange. Liz touched it, sliding it around her finger over and over again. Next to her, Chad released a snore, and she looked over at him to see if he would be shaken from his sleep. He rolled onto his side and turned, his back toward her as Liz pulled her knees up to her chest and looked down at the ring. In the dark of the night, she could still see the shimmering crystals of the diamond. If she had to choose the perfect diamond, this would be it. Though it was more lavish than she would have preferred, it caught her breath every time she looked down at it.

Chad made a noise, and Liz checked on him once more. He was still sound asleep, his light snoring proving just that. Liz tossed the covers back and slid out of bed. It was no surprise that they ended up in bed together to end the night. It was what happily engaged couples would do, right? No shame in that. She sunk into the chair across from the bed and stared at the ring. The light of the moon shone through her bedroom window.

When Liz's mom first told her about Chad, she was adamant that she didn't need to be set up with anyone and could easily find her match. As she headed into college, she looked forward to exploring men in the most natural of ways, expecting that she would date around. After all, it was the college experience, and according to her friends, a must to get through every exam. *You'll want this time to hook up and not have anything too serious.* It was every-thing, they said to her. But her mother had different ideas. It didn't help that her father seemed to agree.

When she met Chad, she forgot that her mother had anything to do with the setup. Their chemistry was off the charts, and he was the epitome of what she wanted. He was tall, tanned, handsome, and had a personality that even surpassed his looks. He was charming, genuine, and funny. He also had a very endearing smile. She always knew that she would make it through four years of college, and then they would talk about life ambitions and where they were headed. He was older by four years, so he was always waiting for her to get out of school.

Chad always dreamed of having his life mapped out for him and owning his own company by the age of twenty-five. He exceeded those expectations by making it at twenty-three, and it developed into the big conglomerate it became known as. Yet, work took a toll on him, and Liz quickly realized that it might be the most important thing in his life, especially when he disregarded her hopes, dreams, and desires. But it always came back to love. In her heart, she knew she did love Chad, and she always would. Putting the ring on her finger was something that made sense. But how was it possible for something to feel right yet so wrong simultaneously?

Liz touched the diamond and heaved a sigh. She got up from her bed and went over to the jewelry box. Chad was still sleeping, to her knowledge, and she dropped the ring into the top of her box. She couldn't continue to wear it without knowing if it really belonged on her finger.

"Baby?"

Liz froze as she closed her jewelry box. She turned to find him shifting in the bed. He pulled himself up and scanned the room until their eyes locked. A small smile grazed his lips.

"Get that beautiful body over here," he quietly said.

Liz walked over to the bed and slid in next to him, her body brushing against his. "What were you doing out of this bed?" He had a teasing grin that played on his lips as his hand brushed over her shoulder.

"Had to go to the restroom, then realized my jewelry box was open. I'm back here now." She moved in, touching her lips to his. It sounded like a plausible explanation. The way he kissed her proved he even believed it. As she moved into him, his hand reaching around for the nape of her neck, worry settled back inside of her. What if taking the ring was the biggest mistake of her life?

CHAPTER FOUR

Liz

Did time always tick by so slowly? Liz checked her watch for what felt like the fiftieth time; only thirty seconds had passed. She leaned back in the chair and crossed her legs, exasperated by the anxiety that was building inside of her.

She had gotten to the hospital an hour before her shift. That was on her. She knew that no one would be there, not even the chief medical officer. After all, he didn't need to fear the worst, that he would be unemployed by the end of a conversation. Liz checked her watch again and shook her head. Another ten seconds passed. Time was moving at a snail's pace, and she couldn't stand the thought of waiting another minute.

However, it wasn't just a minute Liz needed to wait. By her calculations, she had at least fifteen minutes left to think of the responses she would lay out to her superiors. *I know I was late to work, but I'm sorry.* Or, *I thought helping the patient was the best option. I apologize.* Finally ending with, *I need this job. I'm about to get married.* She mentally groaned. She wasn't going to say that last part. She couldn't even wear the ring; no one would be the wiser.

Liz was relieved that Chad hadn't noticed she wasn't wearing the ring. While she was pleasantly surprised, it did concern her. Wouldn't he have wanted to note the ring that he had placed on her finger just ten hours earlier?

The door opened, startling Liz. "Ms. Fletcher?"

She looked up to see Brian Chandler, the director of nursing, standing there. He held a generous smile on his lips, which pained her even more. He was going to be happy helping her out the door. To him, she was only a number. Liz swallowed the lump in her throat and stood up, following him back into the conference room.

"We didn't mean to leave you out here so long. Have a seat."

"That's all right," Liz said. *I was just practicing what I wanted to say and now feel like I might barf. But don't worry about me.* She sat down in a seat that faced not only him but Brenda.

"Hello, Elizabeth," she said. Brenda was Liz's supervisor on the pulmonology floor. The woman who had given her the opportunity to work at Capmed straight out of her clinicals. Elizabeth nodded to her. Of course she would be there. After all, Liz was being fired for not being to work on time. Brenda had a huge stake in losing an employee. Perhaps she would even be the one giving her the pink slip. Liz started to wring her hands even more, nerves seeping inside of her.

"One more will be joining us soon. He's just running a little late," Brian started, grabbing the seat next to Brenda.

Who else could be coming? Liz couldn't fathom who needed to be there. Wasn't it hard enough for two people to ridicule her? And now she was going to be faced with a third?

"We can get started. I know we haven't formally been introduced to one another," Brian continued. "I try to get out there and meet all the staff, but unfortunately, time just doesn't allow that. I leave it up to the individual managers to mold the employees into what Capmed is today and will continue to be. And we all take that job seriously. If we feel someone needs to be shifted through the hospital or permanently removed, then we have to take those actions and put them into motion."

The blood drained from Liz's face. She slumped back into the seat, then quickly sat up straighter. She couldn't look like a slouch right now. She had to take this news and try to rework it in her favor. She wasn't a quitter, and if that meant groveling, then groveling was what they would get.

"May I quickly say something?" she asked, her heart rapidly beating in her chest.

Brian's eyebrows narrowed, and he nodded. "Of course."

"I know that I shouldn't have been late. I know that I should have gotten someone else to help out in the ER and firmly insisted that I had to get to my department. However, when I saw the pain in that girl's eyes, I couldn't ignore it. That is my mistake, and I am deeply sorry."

Brian glanced over at Brenda, and he frowned. Brenda's eyes shot up in surprise, but that didn't stop Liz from going on.

"If there's anything I can do to change the outcome of this meeting, I will gladly do it. If you want to put me on probation, then so be it. I will take some time off and—"

"Let me stop you right there," Brian said, putting out his hand toward Liz.

She chomped back the words she was going to say, frustrated that he wasn't allowing her to plead her case. It was over and done. She had to take it and hope that they would be willing to give her a recommendation. That sounded like a laugh, though.

The back door opened to the conference room, and Liz followed the man who entered with her eyes as he grabbed a seat on the other side of Brenda. "My apologies I wasn't here sooner," he started. "Did I miss anything?"

Brian coughed, clearing his throat. "Not much, really." He turned his full attention to Liz. "I don't want you to continue because I think you might have the wrong idea about this meeting today. This is Frank Kinner. He's the supervisor of the ER. We're not terminating you, Elizabeth. We're asking you if we can shift you from the pulmonology department to the emergency department."

Liz's jaw dropped. "What?"

Brenda nodded. "As an organization, we know that the best thing to do for our new employees is for them to take up roles they are best suited for. We're wondering whether the ER would be a better fit for you than the pulmonology ward."

"I don't understand. I thought I was being…" Her words trailed off, and she sighed. "But I was late."

"And for a good reason," Brian said. "The girl whom you brought attention to had a concussion and needed to be monitored. Your quick actions might have prevented an adverse outcome."

Liz didn't know what to say. "I'm just surprised."

He smirked. "I can see that, but we all feel that the ER

would benefit an employee who has such compassion as you have shown."

"So, what do you say?" Frank asked. "Will you join our team?"

Liz's jaw fell open. When her gaze went to Brenda, she beamed like a proud mother bear. "There's a waiting list of staff that would like to transfer to the ER. This is truly a great honor they are offering you here. We hate to see you go, but we couldn't possibly stand in your way."

Liz didn't know if she wanted to burst into tears or laughter. Either way, though, she couldn't believe how hard she had been on herself, and now she had options. She could take it or leave it, but it was up to her.

Liz stood outside the cafeteria, pacing back and forth, waiting for Hanna to appear. They had decided to meet up for lunch, but as time passed, Liz feared that her lunch would be over before Hanna even got there. Then, she spotted her turn the corner, and their eyes met.

Liz rushed up to Hanna. "Sorry I'm late," Hanna groaned. "Another hectic day in the ER."

"And I'm looking forward to that," Liz said.

Hanna turned to her, cocking up one eyebrow. "Meaning?"

"That's what they wanted to discuss with me at the meeting this morning. It turns out they're not firing me. Instead, they offered me a position in the ER. I'm going to be working with you. I start tomorrow."

Hanna squealed and tossed her arms around Liz's neck.

"You have no idea how thrilled I am. Not just for you, but for me." She giggled, parting from the embrace and turning back to the cafeteria line, quickly moving forward to the next spot in line. "It's exhausting, most times. I can't even lie about that, but it does bring enjoyment knowing that you're healing these people who are in bad shape."

She held out a tray, which Liz grabbed. "Are you stoked?"

"Of course," Liz replied. "I mean, I thought I was getting fired. But I got to meet with Frank, and he seems like a good guy."

"Frank is the best. I've been in three different departments thus far, and I've had four, no, five, different supervisors in the ER. I would say Frank is my favorite. I'll take the fried chicken and noodles," she said, stepping up to the woman at the food line.

Liz skimmed her eyes over the choices for the day and settled on the bacon cheeseburger and fries. They both went to the cashier and paid, then found a table.

"It's great news, though. I knew they weren't going to fire you." Hanna smirked as she dug into her potatoes.

"I wish I had been as confident as you were. It would have saved a lot of hassle and worry." Liz took a big bite of her sandwich. She looked past Hanna and saw Marisa coming from the cafeteria line and heading over to a table. Marisa raised her hand and waved, causing Liz to respond with the same.

Hanna looked over at Marisa, then back to Liz. "You know Marisa?" she asked.

"Met for a bit yesterday in the breakroom. I told her how I was most likely getting the boot." Liz snickered, taking another bite of her sandwich.

"Well, you might want to get to know her," Hanna stated. "Won't find a better confidante than her. She's a good person. We went to college together, then did our externships here. The rest is history, but I would advise that you seek her out whenever you need to."

"Is that so?" Liz asked, taking a drink of her bottled water while Hanna continued.

"In the ER, there are plenty of times when lab tests get fucked up. If you're friends with Marisa, she'll have your back. Just hunt her down, and she'll be there for you."

Liz frowned. "So, what I hear you say is, you use her?"

Hanna laughed through a bite of her chicken. "That sounds so demeaning when you say it like that. I'm just saying Marisa is a good one, and you'll want to keep her happy, so don't irritate her."

Liz shook her head and looked over to Marisa as she chatted with a man at a table on the other side of the cafeteria. She thought about the way Marisa had patiently listened to her the other day when she was rambling about her work troubles. The entire time, Marisa had given Liz her full attention. Then she had talked Liz through her anxiety until she felt better.

She peeled her eyes away from Marisa, her stomach warming. "Marisa doesn't strike me as someone who gets irritated. At least not in the ten minutes I spoke with her."

Hanna's smile widened. "You're right. I'm just kidding, but just remember that you can typically count on her."

"Good to know," Liz softly replied, continuing to eat her lunch as time quickly progressed.

Halfway into lunch, Hanna's phone beeped, and she looked down at it and shook her head. "And my lunch is over. Gotta run. Emergency. Enjoy your lunch today, because tomorrow things will never be the same." She winked, then grabbed her lunch, which had barely been touched, and hurried from the table.

Liz went back to her food and kept her eyes down, lost in thought.

"This seat taken?"

She looked up to find Marisa's mesmerizing, caring eyes gazing down at her. She wore her normal lab coat, but Liz became too aware of how it hugged Marisa's waist, accentuating her hips. Marisa's hair was done in a messy bun, a few strands trailing the nape of her neck. Liz had the sudden urge to reach up and sweep the hairs away and run her thumb along Marisa's jawline.

Liz quickly shook her head, pulling her tray closer to her, giving Marisa more room. She avoided eye contact. What was wrong with her? She shouldn't be thinking such thoughts about Marisa or any woman. She was with Chad—engaged to him. She picked at her food, trying to calm her insides. She was probably just lonely and so exhausted her mind was doing silly things.

"So?" Marisa said, her light, cheerful voice making Liz's heart flutter.

"So…?"

Marisa rolled her eyes, then laughed. "The meeting this morning. How'd it go?"

A light, tingling sensation filled Liz's chest. She hadn't expected Marisa to recall their conversation from the previous day, let alone care enough to inquire about it. But, as Marisa stared at her wide-eyed, waiting to hear all about it, Liz knew

Hanna's words were true. For the first time in a long time, Liz felt seen. Heard. Chad hated to talk about work and get into "heavy" topics, but Marisa seemed to genuinely care and want to offer support.

Liz wanted nothing more than to get to know Marisa. Talk with her. Be near her warmth. But she was still engaged to Chad and needed to remember that. She only wanted Marisa to be a friend. Nothing more. She just needed to keep her crazy thoughts in check.

CHAPTER FIVE

Marisa

A s Marisa sat down and Liz started telling her about her earlier meeting, Marisa waited for Liz to take a breath. She smiled and shook her head as that break eventually came. "I believe I told you that you weren't going to get fired. Didn't I?"

Liz nodded. "So, this is the I-told-you-so speech?"

"Nah." Marisa laughed. "I won't go that far. But I'm happy for you. Sounds like a great opportunity."

"Yeah, and they said that I would have some say in helping to implement an easier check-in process."

Liz suddenly frowned, staring down at her food.

"Then why the long face?" Marisa asked.

Liz shrugged, her eyes still downward. She picked up a fry, then dropped it, then picked it up again, then dropped it. Marisa wasn't a mind reader, but she could tell there was definitely something bothering her.

"Saw you over here with Hanna," Marisa started. Still, Liz didn't seem to look up, so Marisa tried again. "Hanna is one of the good ones. We went to college together and became instant friends."

"She said the same," Liz mumbled.

"That doesn't have anything to do with the concern I see spread all over your face, does it?"

Liz looked up, arching an eyebrow in response. "Why would Hanna have anything to do with my concerns?"

"I don't know. Maybe the fact that Hanna works in the ER and you're clearly friends with her, so you might be feeling that you're coming in and taking over her turf." Marisa took a sip of her soda and shrugged. "Just a thought."

"Well, I am friendly with Hanna. We hardly know each other, though." Liz touched her fry again, then scrunched up her forehead before dropping it. She had been playing with her food for nearly five minutes, not bothering to eat.

Finally, Liz cocked an eyebrow, then sighed. "You're rather perceptive, I would say." She finally picked up the fry and put it into her mouth, then pushed her tray to the side. "I'm just getting to know her, and I don't want to ruin that by getting in the way too much."

Marisa took a drink, not completely convinced that was the reason for Liz's concern. Something else seemed to be on her mind, but she didn't want to pry. "I'll give you some advice. You don't have to worry about Hanna in that respect. She doesn't get caught up in gossip or drama. If I know her, and I'm sure I do, she's just thankful to have more help in the ER."

Marisa shook her head. "She'll know you aren't trying to come in and take over. I can tell she respects you. That's a good thing. Don't go worrying about something that probably won't happen. Besides, look at this morning. You were convinced you were on the chopping block, and yet, look at you now." She smiled, hoping that would relieve some of the stress that was running through Liz's mind.

Liz returned the smile and it lit up her whole face. Marisa's breath caught. Even with minimal makeup and a messy ponytail, Liz was stunning. Her lips glistened from a light dusting of ChapStick, and she thought of leaning across the table to taste it.

Marisa looked away, forcing her mind to focus on their conversation and not get lost thinking inappropriate thoughts at work. "But I don't envy you. The ER is no joke. Good luck with that one." She sipped her soda and watched Liz's wide eyes soften.

"That concerns me a bit," Liz replied. "Just a tiny bit." She held up her fingers, pinching her thumb and index finger, and Marisa nodded.

"But congratulations. I'm sure you'll do amazing. You seem to be the type of person who really cares. That's the most attractive quality in a woman." Her jaw dropped as she instantly realized the mistake she made. "I mean, in a nurse. Not attractive, but a good quality. Not that you're not..." She let her words fade so she didn't keep rambling.

A lovely shade of pink spread across Liz's cheeks as she stared at Marisa for a moment, lips parted. Then she shoved a forkful of food into her mouth, chewing while avoiding eye contact. "Right. And I do care. But that's also an issue when I care too much. I take others' feelings into account more than my own."

Marisa released a breath, happy they had moved on from her Freudian slip. She hated when that happened, especially when she was desperately trying to convince herself she wasn't attracted to Liz. She couldn't be. Liz was *way* too young. They could be friends, but that was all. Yet, when Liz stared at her with those deep hazel eyes, it flubbed up Marisa's mind. Her eyes drew Marisa in, confusing her in ways that no other woman had done in the past year.

Marisa stood, grabbing her soda. The longer she stayed, the more prone she'd be to slipups. "If you need anything, labs or whatever, just let me know. I have to run."

"See ya," Liz said, barely looking in her direction as Marisa scurried off.

Marisa wasn't feeling like her normal self today. One more second around Liz and she might not have been able to pull herself away. Getting lost in those eyes was making her forget everything she promised herself. She escaped into the elevator and waited for the doors to close before falling back against the wall. *She's too young for you, Marisa. You aren't ready for a relationship, anyhow.* If she could repeat that mantra—really drill it into her head— then she might be able to make it.

Liz didn't look any older than twenty-four. That was an eighteen-year difference, which meant Marisa would carry the weight of teaching Liz too much about relationships. Dating someone so young was absurd. When she was ready to start dating again, she would need someone with more life experience. Someone emotionally mature. She didn't yet know Liz well enough, but all women her age weren't emotionally ready for solid, long-term relationships. She had learned that the hard way. Never again.

The elevator opened, and she stepped onto the diagnostic floor and headed to the lab department. Samantha sat at the front desk, her legs propped up, and she had an apple in one hand and a book in the other. She pulled her legs down and swiveled to look at Marisa.

"Didn't mean to interrupt," Marisa mumbled.

"You're back early from lunch. Cafeteria must've been dead." Samantha closed her book and took a bite of her apple as Marisa grabbed the empty chair next to her desk.

"Something like that. What are you reading?"

Samantha grabbed her book and held it up. Marisa smirked when she read the title. "What's so funny?" Samantha pouted, tossing her book to the side.

"Harry Potter? That surprises me. I thought you'd be more about romance." Marisa shrugged. "Not to say there's anything wrong with Harry Potter or anything. Frankly, never read it, but it's surely popular."

"It's my younger cousin's. She let me borrow it over the weekend. Not bad, but I'm sure not everyone's cup of tea, either." Samantha looked down at her computer screen, a slight frown etched on her face. "But, speaking of romance," she started.

Marisa tilted her head and stared at her. She couldn't wait to hear what she had to say. Two lines had formed at the edges of Samantha's hairline, and her nose was scrunched up. Her dark eyes shifted back and forth, from Marisa to the lobby door and back. "There's this guy I'm seeing."

Marisa nodded, leaning back in her chair and crossing her

legs as she waited patiently for Samantha to continue. Marisa liked giving advice, and if it didn't involve her own love life, she was all in. Besides, there were moments when Marisa felt like the mother hen to the young employees. It gave her a sense of purpose, and she was all for helping whenever she could.

"And I like him," Samantha continued, "but I'm starting to have feelings for a coworker. Feelings that I don't quite know how to handle. I've never felt like this before. It's all sorts of confusing and really unexpected, considering who it is." She lifted her eyes timidly to gauge Marisa's reaction.

How juicy! Marisa wasn't normally one for gossip, but she really needed the distraction today. "Is it Alan? I see you two chatting a lot and I know he's single."

"No, not Alan. This person is—"

"Wait. Dr. Harris? Even I'll admit that he's a nice-looking man."

Samantha smirked. "No, not Dr. Harris," she said softly. After chewing her lower lip for a moment, she locked eyes with Marisa and inhaled sharply, opening her mouth.

Before Samantha could continue, the door to the lab opened, halting the conversation. They both turned to look at the woman who walked in.

"The name is Beth Yancy. I have a one o'clock appointment. I know I'm early."

"That's all right," Marisa said, standing up from her chair. "Samantha will get you all checked in, and I'll be out for you in a minute."

She grabbed the order from the woman and took it to the backroom. Samantha's words had her on the edge of her seat, and the last thing she wanted was to leave without getting the full details, but work came first. She would have to remember to ask Samantha more about it later because not knowing who the mystery man who had captured Samantha's interest was would drive her crazy. At least she would have some distraction from what she was feeling for Liz. Anything to keep from thinking about those hazel eyes.

———

Marisa stepped out from the back, relieved that she finally had a lull in the afternoon. It was going to be short-lived, as she was the only laboratory manager on the schedule and their next appointment was in ten minutes, but it was long enough to hear more of Samantha's story.

"Sorry we haven't been able to talk," Marisa said, approaching her from behind.

"That's okay. It happens." Samantha swiveled in her seat to face her. "I'm wondering if maybe it's too much to lay out on you, though. I don't want you to think I'm getting overly dramatic or anything—just something I need to get off my chest. I'm not trying to be one of those teenagers who are all drama llama. You know what I mean?"

Marisa tilted her head and laughed. "Not exactly. Never heard that phrase before, but you don't have to worry. I don't think of you that way. You've always proven yourself to be much more mature for your age."

"Really?"

Marisa nodded.

Samantha's shoulders relaxed. "I'm really glad you think so. It makes our age difference seem less, right?"

Marisa took the seat next to her. "Well, we're friends. You know I'll always be here for you. Don't ever fear you're giving me too much. I've been around teens and tweens, so I can assure you whatever you have to say won't come across as overly dramatic."

If the drama ever got too much, she wasn't ever afraid to take a step back and tell someone that they needed to lay it on someone else. With Samantha, though, she had this over-whelming feeling that Samantha needed Marisa's help. She wasn't about to turn her away.

Things were harder for Samantha since she felt forced to continue living at home with her parents as she worked to save up money and move out. Marisa knew Samantha had dreams of going to college but wasn't presently in the position to make that happen. She had an unusual living arrangement, having multiple generations under one roof, but it eased their financial burden. Marisa admired that their family was so close.

"What's going on?" Marisa leaned back in her chair, watching Samantha.

"Um, well, about this coworker, I can't shake my feelings. They've been getting stronger the past couple of months, and I feel like if I don't say something, I'm going to implode."

"And you don't have any feelings for your boyfriend?" Marisa asked, urging the conversation forward.

"Well, he's not really a boyfriend. Just a guy I see every once in a while. Nothing too big to share there, but no. I don't have these feelings for him."

"Well, I can tell you that you'll ultimately hurt him in the process if you're not honest," Marisa replied. "So, for one thing, you need to make sure you're clear with him on what your intentions are. As for the other guy, you have to tell him, too."

"You see…" Samantha started.

The door opened and Marisa turned to face their next patient. "Have a seat, and we'll be right with you." Marisa grabbed Samantha's hand and pulled her into the backroom. "She can wait a few minutes. She's early anyhow. We can talk easier back here."

"Right," Samantha whispered. She shifted from one foot to the next, and Marisa saw the uneasiness in her eyes, even apprehension. She reached out and touched her arm.

"You look nervous. Is this coworker someone you shouldn't see? Like a guy who's much older than you? Or maybe someone much younger? Or a guy your parents wouldn't approve of? Whatever the case, I think you need to have a serious conversation with your mom and dad. They are your parents, and you should honor and respect them—most of all, love them—but they can't dictate your whole life. Remember that."

Exasperation showed on Samantha's face as she shook her head. "It's not that. It's just—"

"Hey, Marisa?"

Marisa turned to see Liz stepping into the room where they were. "Liz! What's going on? Everything all right?" Marisa stepped away from Samantha and toward Liz.

Liz looked down at the paper in her hand, then back up to Marisa. "I just was looking for you. I have an urgent blood draw from the pulmonology department. Dr. Barr asked me to get a rush on it. I see you're busy and all, but can I at least drop it off to you? If you could come to the floor at your earliest convenience and get the patient taken care of, that'd be great."

Marisa turned to Samantha, who shot Liz an angry glare and then walked toward the door. "I'll let the patient know that we'll be a few minutes late." Then she stormed off.

Wonder what that was about?

Marisa turned back to Liz. "Let Dr. Barr know that I'll grab my supplies and be right up."

"Thank you so much!" Liz gave a smile, then turned on her heel and left the backroom. Marisa walked out behind her and toward Samantha, who was typing something on her computer.

"Sorry for the interruption," Marisa whispered so the patient wouldn't hear her. "We can quickly finish our conversation if you'd like. I feel like you were just about to tell me anyway."

Samantha looked up and shook her head, her voice tense. "It's all right. Nothing to say, really. We'll discuss it later." She went back to her work as Marisa went to get the supplies for Liz's patient. She hesitated at the door and tossed a look over her shoulder. They would have to have that talk soon, and she would do everything she could to help Samantha out.

CHAPTER SIX

Liz

The minute Liz started working in the emergency room, she felt things improving with her employment at the hospital. She felt like she suddenly had a purpose, which was more than she could say when she first started working at Capmed. She had now worked at the hospital for over a month and was finally finding her own pace.

She grabbed the chart from the pile, sighing as she looked at the pile. She still had so many ideas of how they could triage the patients, but there was scarce time to figure out how to do it. In due time, she would see if they could make it a priority.

"Donovan?" she called out, stepping to the corner of the desk. A woman approached Liz with her young son. Liz smiled at the woman, then looked down at her child. "My name is Liz, and I'll be taking care of you today. Follow me."

The boy hovered next to his mother, his small hand in hers as they followed after Liz. Liz stopped at the scale and motioned for him to get on.

He was unsteady getting onto the scale. His mom had to hold his hand and whisper a few words of encouragement. Within seconds, the digital readout on the scale flashed his weight.

"Very good. Go ahead and go into that room right there, and I'll be right with you." Liz smiled at the mom, then stayed in the hallway and read through the previous history from that appointment. *Bloody nose. Bruising for unknown reasons.* Now add instability. While Liz wasn't a doctor, she didn't like the symptoms already.

She entered the room and shut the door behind her, addressing the mother. "Now, tell me, what brings you in here today?" While Donovan was only six years old, Liz didn't feel he would be able to reiterate his need to be in the emergency room on that Friday afternoon.

"We went to see our family doctor last week," his mother started. "He was experiencing a low fever, and he had a few bloody noses that we found odd. They just came on so suddenly. Then we found some bruises on his legs. We thought he just fell. Boys fall after all, and he goes to kindergarten all day. So we didn't think much of it. But the bruises didn't seem to want to go away. Our doctor ordered X-rays of his legs and they didn't show any fractures. But today we saw this." She pulled back his shirt, revealing his elbow, where there was a bruise the size of a quarter.

She shrugged. "He says he doesn't recall falling, and we have some concerns. Or, at least I do, that maybe something is going on at his school." She sighed. "There's no way of proving it, though." She then felt his forehead and nodded. "But now he has a fever. It's running just over a hundred."

Liz grabbed the thermometer and took the boy's temperature from his forehead. "One hundred point three," Liz said, quickly documenting that.

"And he says he's nauseous."

Liz looked down at her folder and wrote that down, then looked back up. "How long have you noticed the fever?"

"Just today. The bruise, this morning."

Liz grabbed hold of his wrist to take his pulse, which was rapid, going faster than she would have liked. She wondered if it had something to do with him having to sit for a while waiting to be seen. She documented the pulse and knelt in front of him. "Do you feel sick right now?" she asked.

He nodded. "Sore."

"Where are you sore, bud?"

He touched his head, then his knees.

"Stomach hurts," he said. He scrunched up his nose and rubbed his stomach.

"We'll get you taken care of." She ruffled his hair and stood up. "I'm going to grab the doctor, and he'll be right in with you."

"Thank you, ma'am," his mother replied. "I'm Victoria, by the way."

Liz smiled and turned to her. "Call me, Liz. Won't be too long." She left the room and logged onto the computer. There was one thing that did concern her, and it was the possibility of him being abused. However, it didn't account for his fever and the pain in his head and knees. More serious conditions had to be considered: idiopathic thrombocytopenic purpura, and even leukemia.

When she spotted Dr. Wesley, she walked over to him. "My patient in room three?" he asked.

"Yeah, it's a child."

He looked over the chart and nodded.

"I was the doctor that examined him last time. It's a shame he's back." He slid the pen behind his ear and shook his head.

"So, the mother says she has a concern that maybe his school is abusing him. Because of the bruising and stuff." Liz nibbled on her lip. "But how can you be sure that it's not the family? Like, maybe the family is just pointing fingers."

He nodded. "It can be a concern, for sure. I'll have a thorough talk with her. If I have concerns, I'll ask the social worker to come by."

"Dr. Wesley?" Victoria asked when they were nearing the end of his examination. "I was hoping you and I could speak alone for a moment?"

Liz shot a look to Dr. Wesley as he nodded.

"Donovan? Would you like to go with me and get a Jell-O?" Liz asked, turning to him.

His eyes lit up, and he eagerly nodded. Liz lifted him down from the bed, and they walked out of the room hand in hand. Liz escorted him to the nurses' station, where there wasn't anyone around. "What's your favorite flavor?" she asked, lifting him onto the counter and moving around to the refrigerator.

"Cherry?"

Donovan nodded, and she pulled one out of the fridge.

"You're in luck. It's the last one." She grabbed a spoon, then opened it for him. He took a bite, and his smile widened. He grew silent, focused on his eating. Liz leaned against the counter and just watched him. Looking at him, you wouldn't be able to tell he wasn't feeling well, other than the fact that his skin looked so pale.

She reached up and pressed her hand to his forehead, and he rolled his eyes. "Mommy does that all the time."

She laughed. "Well, I'm sure your mommy is just worried. It's what mommies do."

"Do you have any kids?" he asked, still eating from his Jell-O cup.

"No, I don't. But I know from experience with my own mommy. I might be much older than you, but mommies never stop worrying about their children."

"When I'm a daddy, I'll be the same." He proudly looked up at her, and she smiled brightly.

"I'm sure you will." She ruffled her fingers through his hair and frowned at the heat that radiated off him. "How are you feeling now?" she asked.

He nodded. "Better. This was really good." He took the last bite from his cup, and she took the empty cup and spoon from him.

"I'm pretty tired," he said.

Liz nodded in concern as she led him back to the ER room. "You are? All the time?" she asked.

He nodded, then looked down at his hands. "I don't like to say that because that makes Mommy sad, too."

"I understand that, bud. But you have to tell when you're feeling not like yourself. If you're feeling blah, then you need to let your mommy know everything. And you need to let your doctor know everything."

"And you," he said. "I need to tell you."

She smiled and nodded. "Now you've got it."

"I like you." His eyes went wider.

"I'll tell you a secret," Liz whispered. "I like you, too."

He giggled, and she was surprised when he pulled her into a hug. Liz allowed the hug to linger. While they embraced, Dr. Wesley walked out of the room and motioned for her to bring him back inside.

"Looks like they're ready for us," Liz said. As they entered, she fought the urge to cry. What was it about this situation that tore at her strings more than anything else? The fact that he was a child, no doubt, but something else was pressing on her, causing her to want to break down.

Dr. Wesley helped Donovan back onto the bed and then took a seat on the stool in the room. "Donovan, stick out your tongue for me, please."

Donovan did that, and Dr. Wesley pushed his chair up to the bed.

"Say ahhh…" Donovan obliged as Dr. Wesley looked down his throat. He nodded, then scooted back from him. "I'm a little worried about the bruising. As for the bloody noses, the air has been dry, so I'm prescribing some nose drops. This could all be part of a viral infection. I recommend plenty of fluids and lots of rest. Most importantly, you'll need to follow up with your family doctor in a day or two. But if you're not able to, you're welcome to bring him back here again. Do you have any questions for me?"

Victoria shook her head, and her eyes were bright red as if she'd been crying. Liz's heart tore at that sight; she couldn't fathom the pain a parent would have knowing their child wasn't feeling well.

"All right. Don't hesitate to come back or give us a call if you need anything."

Liz knelt in front of Donovan. "You are a special little man. Don't ever forget that."

Donovan nodded, then wrapped his arms around her again before pulling away. He had perked up a little, and even managed a faint smile.

She ruffled his hair with her hand, then stepped back as she left the room with Dr. Wesley. Dr. Wesley glanced in her direction as they stopped outside the door, and she shook her head.

"I can see the emotions swirling inside of you," he said. "Are you okay?"

She shrugged, then swallowed the lump in her throat. "Do you just think it's some virus that needs to run its course?"

He looked away from her, and she kept her eyes straight on him until he looked back at her and shrugged. "I think so, based on his signs and symptoms. His throat was a tad irritated. He's nauseous. He has a fever. If there are more concerns, we can get our social worker to reach out to the family. Was there something in particular you had in mind?"

"I was worried about leukemia," Liz muttered. She slipped her hands into her pockets and sighed. "My brother had leukemia as a child. But, if memory serves me, that's diagnosed by a blood test, and I don't see anywhere where one was ordered."

"It's possible," Dr. Wesley responded. "That's why I urged them to follow up with their family doctor or come back here if things persist."

"I don't understand." Her voice went up a couple of notches. "I don't mean to suggest that you're not doing everything you should. I know you're the doctor and all, but I don't see why you wouldn't do that first thing and rule it out."

Dr. Wesley crossed his arms. "Emergency medicine is a constant challenge. We don't want to miss serious conditions but we don't have the time and resources to work every patient up as thoroughly as we'd like. On top of that, we have to play a delicate balancing act in which we take responsibility for the patients' welfare without interfering with the relationship they have with their family physicians."

"Okay. I get it."

Liz looked away from him, tears threatening to fall. She was worried for Donovan. This was just one thing that was pulling her back to her past, reminding her of the heartache that her family had endured for nearly three years. She glanced back at the little boy through the doorway, fearing for his future.

"Excuse me." She fled before she finally broke down. She couldn't let Dr. Wesley or Donovan see her like that.

Hanna was passing by and noticed Liz's distraught state. "Liz? What's wrong?" she asked, rushing up to her.

"Sorry. I have to take a break," Liz said, pushing past Hanna to the elevator. She jammed her finger against the button. When the doors opened, she saw that someone was already inside.

"Liz!" Marisa exclaimed just before Liz rushed inside and collapsed against the wall of the elevator.

Marisa reached up and pressed the emergency stop button. Liz wanted to collapse in tears somewhere dark and quiet where no one would see her, but knowing Marisa was here was comforting. And now no one would bother them. "Thank you," she said softly.

"What's wrong?" Marisa pulled her into her arms, and Liz couldn't hold back anymore. As she rested her head against Marisa's shoulder, a flood of tears fell down her cheeks. She cried for her brother, who had succumbed to his illness, and she cried for Donovan, whose future might be uncertain. She just hoped that Donovan and his family wouldn't have to experience the same pain she had.

Through all of the painful memories clouding Liz's thoughts, Marisa was there—a soft, reassuring embrace Liz hadn't realized she'd been so long without.

LIZ PULLED HER ENGAGEMENT RING OUT OF HER JEWELRY BOX and slipped it back on her finger. Since she was headed out on a date with Chad, she had to make an effort to show him that she wanted this engagement to work.

She heaved a sigh as she looked at herself in the mirror. The problem was, she wasn't in the mood to go out to a concert or take a romantic stroll along a pier, which were the two things Chad had on tonight's agenda. After spending the morning crying at the hospital, she was ready to put on her lounge pants and crawl into bed.

Her phone rang, and she looked down at the number. She didn't recognize the number on the screen, but it was a Chicago area code, so she answered. "Hello?"

"Liz? It's Marisa."

Her heart sped up, butterflies entering her stomach. "Um,

hi. How'd you get my number?" Liz sat down on the edge of her bed.

"I, well, I just, I'm sorry if this isn't okay. I asked Hanna, and she gave it to me."

She didn't know why Marisa wanted her number, let alone why she was calling on a Friday night, but she couldn't deny how happy she was hearing Marisa's voice. "I see," she slowly replied, her voice slightly husky.

"Is that okay? I mean, I don't want to bother you or anything, but after we saw each other today in the elevator, I just wanted to make sure you were okay."

Liz exhaled and smiled. Marisa was so thoughtful and caring. Liz still had Donovan and her brother heavy on her mind, so she appreciated that Marisa was checking up on her.

She closed her eyes, remembering the warmth of Marisa's embrace in the elevator. Marisa hadn't told her to stop or that she was silly for crying—something Chad often did. She had only held Liz and let her get her emotions out. She had been a blubbering mess, but Marisa didn't once judge her while she was crying. She had just needed to fall apart at that moment, and Marisa had been there to catch her. Since Marisa was an older woman, Liz had felt comforted and assured that everything would be okay. Liz didn't know if that was actually true, but in that moment, it felt true.

Once she had stopped crying, the urge to stay wrapped in Marisa's embrace was so strong that she had lingered a few extra moments.

"Liz? You still there?"

"Yeah."

"I don't mind that Hanna gave you my number. It's nice that you called. I'm sorry I was a mess earlier."

"Don't even worry about that. I can assure you that I've had moments like that at work. Many times I feel like falling to pieces. And it takes a special person to be a nurse, so you never have to shy away from me, Liz. I was just concerned about you. That's all."

A tear escaped Liz's eye, and she flicked it away. "That means a lot to me. Thank you." From someone she didn't know all that well, it meant even more.

Her doorbell rang, signaling that Chad had arrived. "I'm doing well. Well, maybe just okay. I'm holding out hope that Donovan only has a virus and that he'll feel better soon. Coworkers like you will help me to be stronger the next time I have to face a patient who might not get such good news."

Chad rang the doorbell again, and Liz stood up from her bed. "I'm sorry, but I have to go. I really can't thank you enough for calling. I mean that. I appreciate it so much."

Marisa was quiet a moment, then said, "Anytime. We'll talk later."

Liz disconnected the call, staring at Marisa's lingering number on the screen. She already missed hearing her voice. For a split second, she thought of telling Chad she was sick and calling Marisa back so they could talk more. But that was silly. Marisa was just a coworker and she didn't want to bug her. Marisa had already done enough.

After taking a moment to compose herself, she went to the front door to greet Chad.

"Gosh, babe," he said after she opened the door. "Didn't think you were going to answer. You trying to leave me out here in the cold?" He grabbed her hand and pulled her to him, planting a kiss on her lips.

The phone call was still on her mind. If Marisa cared about how she was doing, it would only seem right that her fiancé would share the same thoughts. He wasn't always receptive to her, but now might be a good time to open up. They were engaged, after all. She should be talking to him about the things that worried her. He should be her number one supporter.

"Been an emotional day," she said as she pulled back from the kiss. "So, I was hoping it would be all right if we just stayed in tonight. I'm not feeling like going out and having a good time. Maybe we could talk about my work? I have so much on my mind lately."

He frowned. "Are you serious? I'm dressed up and everything. And you are, too, for that matter. Don't be silly. We'll go out and have a good time." He grabbed her hand and pulled her closer. "I'll make sure you have the time of your life and don't have to think about your crummy day."

He tried to kiss her, but Liz pressed her hand against his chest, pressing him back. "Today, I saw a sick child. And it brought up thoughts of Jeremy when he was ill. So, I'm not in the mood."

He scrunched up his face, his eyes going darker. "I'm sorry about that, but there's nothing you can do, right? I know it was hard, but that's in the past. That doesn't mean you have to stop your life."

Liz's jaw dropped, and she looked away from him. "My brother died from leukemia," she said. She glanced up at him, and he simply nodded. "Just hit me hard today. That's all."

"I don't want you to think I'm a jerk. I know that's rough,

and I'm sorry you had to deal with that. You're going to run into a lot of sick kids at your job. Maybe this is too stressful for you. I told you it might be, didn't I?"

Liz crossed her arms. "It's not too stressful. Just because I'm concerned about a patient doesn't mean I can't handle my work. Just because I have empathy for what the family is going through doesn't mean this isn't the perfect job for me. I love being a nurse. And I have such great coworkers."

He brushed the back of his hand against Liz's cheek, and she pulled back. "You have a kind heart. There's no denying that. That's why I'll be grateful when we're married and this will all be behind you."

"What do you mean by that?" she asked, stepping back and putting space between them.

"Well, when we're married, you'll give up this thought of working. You'll realize that I can support you. You'll just stay home and have babies."

Liz snickered and stepped around him to gain more distance. She knew that he thought she needed to—or perhaps, wanted her to—rely on his money, but telling her to stay at home and pop out babies took it too far. While she wanted children and planned on having as many as God wanted to bless her with, that didn't mean she was ever going to be willing to give up her passion for nursing.

"You know that I chose nursing so I could help people. I've told you that numerous times." She stared at him hard until he nodded. "So, why do you think that once we're married, I'll just decide to give that up?"

"Just trying to help you out, babe. Are you mad at me?"

She made a fist. Was he that oblivious? The look of confusion that played through his eyes said that he just didn't understand. "I don't think I can go out tonight. I'm sorry. I'm not feeling well." She turned and kept her eyes directed elsewhere.

"I didn't mean to upset you. If you want to continue working after we're married we'll talk about that. But I never…" His words broke off as Liz turned back to him. "I didn't mean to assume that you would want to give up the job. I just thought you were doing this job to make ends meet. The stress isn't worth it, is it?"

"Doing your passion and what you're meant to do is always worth it." She looked past him as a tear started to creep down her cheek. "Tonight just isn't a good night."

She pushed past him to the door. As she opened it, she felt glad she hadn't given in to Chad. She tried to walk in without him, but he followed her, shutting the door softly and turning her to face him.

He brushed a finger under her chin, lifting her head to look at him.

"I'm sorry. If you want to work, then you can work. I'm not trying to keep that from you. It's just that you seem so stressed today."

"I'm stressed today," she said. He brushed his thumb along a tear on her cheek. "And I was trying to talk to you about that. But feeling stressed doesn't mean I want to give up my passion."

He nodded and moved in to meet her lips. She stood there, stuck between urging him to leave and allowing the kiss to continue. He agitated her and she didn't understand why he didn't listen to her or respect her desires, especially now that they were engaged. If he kept pushing her to give up her job, it could break them. Was this really the person she should spend the rest of her life with?

But as the kiss deepened, her body responded. She craved comfort at that moment. The day had been so stressful in more ways than one. Not only was the past coming back to haunt her, but feelings for Marisa that she was afraid to explore were stirring in her chest. Ultimately, she relaxed into Chad's embrace, giving her thoughts permission to wander to the one person always on her mind lately.

As he pressed her against the door, she wrapped her arms around his neck, imagining the shapely curves of an older woman surrounding her body with warmth and comfort. A woman who made her heart dance, who listened to her when she needed support. A woman she wished were beside her at that moment more than anyone else.

CHAPTER SEVEN

Marisa

Marisa stepped into the cafeteria and headed straight for the shortest line. While the day had started slowly, it had quickly hit a turn for the worse, and she didn't think she would ever get away to get something to eat. As she stood in the pizza line, she looked over to a table, where she spotted Liz and Hanna eating. Before she could look away, Liz caught her staring. She waved, thoughts of holding Liz drifting through her mind.

Pulling Liz close in the elevator had been a reflex, her heart driving her actions. Liz had needed her at that moment and being able to offer her support—and being wanted—was what Marisa craved. Holding Liz had sent a spark of contentment through her and stirred something deep inside she thought had died with her last relationship.

The woman behind the counter cleared her throat, and Marisa's eyes shot back to the line. She was next. "Sorry," she mumbled. "Pepperoni and sausage, please."

The woman threw her pizza together and put it in the oven as she called over the next customer. Marisa casually looked back over to the table, where Liz now sat alone. She was leaning back, relaxing, sipping on her water, her eyes diverted from where Marisa stood.

"Ma'am," the woman behind the counter spoke. Marisa turned back to find her pizza was ready.

"Oh. That was fast. Thanks."

She grabbed it, pulled a bottle of water from the refrigerator, then paid at the cashier. She hesitated as she watched Liz scroll through her phone, avoiding eye contact. Should she go eat lunch with Liz? Her heart wanted to, but her mind was trying to be reasonable and tell her to stop getting involved. Liz was too young for her. Then Liz looked back up and smiled, her cheeks blushing.

It's just lunch. Nothing more.

Without any more hesitation, she strode to the table. "Hey, Liz."

Liz tucked a stray hair behind her ear. "Hi."

It had been a week since they had last talked, and while Marisa had considered reaching out to her, she pulled back, not wanting to come on too strong. She was still trying to control her feelings, but the more she talked to Liz, the harder it became. Letting herself fall wouldn't end well. Not only was she uncertain if she was ready to date again, but the age gap was too great and she didn't want to jeopardize Liz's job with a workplace romance. If her feelings started to show, others would notice.

After all, the hospital knew where she stood when it came to being a lesbian. So far, Liz still didn't know and she wasn't ready for her to suspect anything.

"Do you want to sit down?" Liz asked.

"I don't want to interrupt if you and Hanna are having lunch together."

"We were but aren't anymore. She had to go back to the ER because Sally's getting ready to leave for the day. So, have a seat."

"Okay." Marisa sat down and opened her water. Her eyes skimmed Liz's loose ponytail and her rounded cheekbones. She had a light application of mascara on and her mouth was curved up in a soft smile. But her eyes looked tired and sunken. The stress of work was still getting to her. Marisa resisted the urge to reach out and take Liz's hand.

"How've you been? I've been thinking of you."

Liz tilted her head, and Marisa tried to cover up her fumble. "I mean, I've been thinking of your patient. Your situation. Not you."

"Gee, that means a lot. Thanks." Liz smirked and took a bite of her sandwich.

Marisa looked down at her pizza. Why was she acting like a nervous teenager around this girl? She was a grown woman and shouldn't find anything awkward about the situation. Sure, Liz was attractive, but she'd been around many beautiful women at the hospital. She had never gotten flustered like this.

"You know what I mean," Marisa mumbled, taking a bite of her pizza. She needed something in her mouth to prevent herself from saying something that would make the situation more awkward.

"I'm teasing. I know what you mean. But, yeah, I'm doing okay. No news is good news, right? At least, that's the motto I'll stand by. I haven't seen the little boy in the ER, so that's good."

"Well, that's something positive to take out of it." Marisa wiped her mouth with her napkin and took a drink. "Anything new otherwise?"

"Not really. But I'm tired of talking about me. What about you? Anything new with you?"

Marisa shrugged and then laughed. "We lead such interesting lives."

After not having had a conversation over the week, one would think there would be something to talk about. Maybe it was the attraction that made Marisa tongue-tied. She was doubtful about that, though. She looked down at her food, then continued with what little she had to go on.

"I'll keep your patient in my prayers," Marisa said. Was that lame? It felt lame. Yet it got a big smile from Liz, causing Marisa's chest to flutter.

"That's really nice. Thank you, and I'm sure both he and his mother would appreciate that."

Marisa nodded, taking a bite of her pizza and catching Liz watching her from the corner of her eye. She put her slice down and wiped her mouth, suddenly feeling self-conscious.

"Do you always do this?" Liz asked.

"Do what?" Marisa arched an eyebrow, thoroughly confused.

"Just have a way of making someone feel like they're being heard?"

Liz's cheeks went red, and she took another bite of her sandwich, but Marisa couldn't turn her gaze away. Not now, when it seemed like they were having a moment. *Am I ready for us to have a moment?*

Liz looked up and smiled. "It feels nice. When I started, I was told if I ever needed anything, you were the one I should go to."

Marisa was taken aback, and she dropped her slice of pizza. "You were told that?"

Liz nodded. "Hanna."

Marisa pondered this, surprised that was the one thing that Liz was told right off the bat.

Liz continued, "So, I know that you must be dependable. I can see that for a fact now."

Marisa knew her cheeks were showing her embarrassment as they quickly warmed up from Liz's words. "Since we're making observations, I'll tell you this: you have a very caring heart."

"You think so?" Liz looked up, locking eyes with Marisa. Marisa could tell by the way Liz was staring that not too many people had told her that. It was a shame because, in her opinion, it couldn't go unnoticed.

"I know so. You're showing so much concern and dedication after only meeting this boy once. I can see it on your face that you're concerned for his well-being. I can assure you that you should never lose that because the worst thing that could happen is to find yourself bitter. I'll tell you, Liz. Nursing isn't for the weak. And if you let it get to you, you will wind up living a rough life, and you don't want that."

Marisa scanned the cafeteria and almost let out a laugh as she caught sight of one of the tables. "See that person over there?"

Liz turned to where Marisa was gazing. "That's Edith, and

she's surely ready for retirement. For some reason, she's holding out, though. That is who you don't want to turn out to be. She comes into work dreading it. She's lost sight of why it was important to work here. So, Liz…"

Liz turned back to look at Marisa, and Marisa smiled, hoping she would get Liz to do the same. Shortly after that, the corners of Liz's mouth lifted. "Promise me you won't be Edith. Seeing death can take a toll on someone, so I need you to promise me."

Liz laughed. "I will do my best not to be an Edith."

"Then you'll do just fine." She took a bite of her pizza, wiping her hands on her napkin and enjoying the soft chortle in Liz's tone when she laughed.

"I definitely needed that laugh," Liz replied.

"Then my work here is done." Marisa smirked, finishing off her pizza. Maybe friendship was what Marisa needed from Liz. Just because the chemistry she felt with her seemed to be surpassing everything she had felt from any other woman over the past year didn't mean she was ready to act on it. Or even should act on it. Just getting to know Liz was enough, wherever that might lead.

"Squeeze your hand for me," Marisa said as she pressed to find the patient's vein. As lab manager, drawing blood wasn't part of her job description, but she enjoyed having patient contact from time to time and always made an effort to maintain her phlebotomy skills.

"Nice and slow. There you go." She grabbed the needle and

inserted it, then filled up the tubes of blood. "Very good. Almost done."

She pulled the tourniquet off, removed the needle, and covered the puncture site with a cotton ball. "You're good to go. I'll send your wife in."

"Thank you!"

She turned from the patient and left with her cart. Out in the hallway, she saw his wife leaning back against the wall. "You're free to go in, Mrs. Jacobs."

"Thank you!"

She went into the room, and Marisa continued down toward the elevator. She had just rounded the corner when Liz almost collided with her from the other way.

"Sorry about that," Liz said.

Before Marisa could continue to the elevator to get back to the lab, Liz stopped next to her. "Here to draw a patient?" she asked. Then she laughed and rolled her eyes. "Pretty stupid question. Of course you're here to draw a patient. You have the lab cart, and you're in the ER."

Marisa chuckled. "No problem, but yep. Just got done. How late are you here 'til?"

"Two!" Liz made a face, then laughed. "You?"

"I'm leaving in an hour. It's been a long and hectic day."

"That it has." Liz continued to move past her. "I'll leave you to get to the elevator. Have a great rest of your night!"

"I will. You, too!" Marisa pressed forward to the elevator, but Hanna headed over to her before she could get to the door.

"Hey," Marisa greeted.

It'd been three days since Liz had mentioned what Hanna had said about being able to rely on Marisa. She considered mentioning it to Hanna, but it didn't quite feel like something she had to bring up. If Hanna felt that way, it was nice, but it'd be awkward to bring it up and make it a big deal. But was it that obvious that Marisa just liked being needed by others? Giving advice?

"So, when should we have those lab results?" Hanna asked.

"I'll put it in when I get upstairs. I leave in an hour, but when the third shift comes in, they should be able to handle getting the results back to you. I'll put a rush on it. Is he spending the night?"

"Yeah, I think we're going to have to get him into a room. Won't be what he wants to hear, but it's probably for the best."

Marisa nodded. "Noted. I'll let them know." She was reaching to press the button to go up when Hanna reached out and stopped her with her hand.

"So, there's something I kind of want to say, and I don't know how to say it. But I'm just going to come out and say it. So, if it gets really weird, pardon me for that."

Marisa gawked, then laughed. "Just come out and say it because it can't be any weirder than what you just said."

Hanna smirked. "Well, that's easier said than done."

Hanna leaned against the elevator and sighed. "Okay, here's the gist. I don't know, and I'm probably reading the signs all wrong, so tell me if you want me to shut up."

"Gladly," Marisa teased. They had known each other long enough to easily be able to tell one another how they felt. That made hearing this conversation different for Marisa. Hanna seemed apprehensive and on edge as she spoke her concern.

"So, Marisa, you know I think you're a great person, and

we've known each other for a long time. In this hospital, by far, you're my best friend."

"Yes, I would say twenty-five years is a long time of knowing a person. But you're freaking me out here a bit."

"Sorry, I'll try to get to the point. You're a good friend, and I care about you. I want you to be happy. I know that things with Shana went south for you and you've taken steps to get through that. So, I'm only saying something because I don't want you to get hurt by any means."

"Hanna, just come out with it because you're confusing me right now."

"Okay. Are you attracted to Liz?"

Marisa stared at her, waiting for Hanna to continue.

"Like sexually attracted, I mean."

Marisa swallowed and tried to maintain her composure. "You've got to be kidding me right now. You wanted to talk about *this*? This has to be a joke. Is there a camera hidden or something?"

She looked around, but when she caught Hanna's gaze, Hanna rolled her eyes. "No? Then there has to be a reason you would ask such a ludicrous question."

"Marisa, it's not all that ludicrous. I see you with her, like you're lurking around or something."

"So, I'm a stalker?" Marisa's jaw dropped, and she looked away from Hanna.

"I didn't mean like that," Hanna quickly replied. "I just think that maybe now you're ready to really open yourself up to love again and wondered if, when you looked at Liz, you got those sorts of feelings. Maybe it's lust, or it's—"

"Stop right there!" Marisa held up her hand. "You realize that she's like twenty-four, right?" Marisa asked.

"Twenty-three," Hanna corrected.

Marisa released a breathless laugh. "Okay, I stand corrected. Even younger. That makes a nineteen-year difference in our ages. Nineteen years, so even if something happened, which I don't want it to, that would be a huge age gap. And certainly, you wouldn't go that route either. So, you're crazy if you think that I would even have any of those feelings for her."

"You can be attracted to who you want to be attracted to," Hanna quietly replied. "Doesn't mean you'd act on them. I just think that it looks like you might be headed in that direction."

"Well, you're wrong," Marisa replied, shaking her head. Despite her outward assertion, inside, she was a mess. Her heart was pounding and her legs felt shaky. If Hanna was picking up on her attraction to Liz, that meant she had already gotten in too deep. "I don't feel anything but a friendship for her, okay? That's all. I would never go there. Ever."

Hanna clapped her hands together. "I'm just glad to hear you say that. Because I care about you both. I don't want you to get caught up in some foolish chase that would only end badly for you. Liz has a boyfriend, and no one wants to see you get your heart crushed, especially me."

As Marisa processed those words, she felt unsteady. Liz had a boyfriend. She was certain that in the times they had talked, that had never come up in the conversation. Not that Liz owed it to her. Still, Marisa would have assumed at some point he would have been mentioned.

"Well, you had the signs wrong. So, you can rest assured that

I'm not sexually attracted to Liz or anyone else for that matter. Feel better?"

Hanna nodded and stepped back from her.

"I really should be getting back to the lab and getting these vials processed. But good talk." She reached up and pressed the button.

"I made it awkward, didn't I?" Hanna asked.

Marisa was still reeling when the door opened. She shook her head, trying to relax her body. "Hey, we've known each other long enough that if you can't make a conversation awkward, then there must be a problem. You're just looking out for us. No one can argue with that, but we're good."

She moved into the elevator and turned to face Hanna. "Have a good night." She let the doors close.

As she took the elevator to her floor, she felt like her gut had been punched and kicked. *Liz had a boyfriend.* She couldn't shake the thought. If she had been on the fence about her true feelings for Liz, everything was crystal clear now. Her feelings ran deep. But now she knew that she needed to pull back, way back, before the tension turned into more than either of them could handle. It was really the best option for her sanity, and going after a straight woman in a relationship was simply wrong.

Marisa returned to the back room and sat down in a waiting chair. Hanna's words had hit her harder than she wanted to admit. Things were going to have to be held in a strictly professional manner, and that was all there was to it. From that point forward, Marisa wasn't going to allow the attraction to get to her.

She just didn't know how hard it would be.

CHAPTER EIGHT

Liz

L iz took a sip of water and sighed as she collapsed into a chair. It was one of the most hectic nights she had faced at the ER since switching departments, and she had faced some pretty hectic times at work. She took another sip of water. She had made a promise she would only leave the ER for a few minutes to relax, then be ready to get back out there. She hoped that Hanna could manage alone, but she had to take a few minutes off her feet. She also needed to clear her head. Everything in her personal life, with Marisa, and with work was overwhelming her and making her mind cloudy. She had made a few dumb mistakes at work today and she couldn't let things like that happen again.

Her phone rang, interrupting her moment of silence, and she groaned. Her first thought was that the ER would say that the two minutes she had was enough. When she grabbed it, though, she saw Chad's number.

Even though she was gripped with thoughts of not answering the call, she hadn't spoken to him in over three days, and that was some record. She had to face him sooner or later.

"Hello?"

"Hey, babe. I wasn't sure you'd answer. Since you're at work, I mean."

"Busy night, so might not be able to talk for too long. But I might have a couple of minutes."

"Alright, then. I'll make it fast. I just wanted to let you know that I have to head to France on the red-eye tonight."

"France? For how long?"

A call beeped in, and she looked at the phone to see Hanna's name. She groaned. She had to take a few more seconds to figure out what was going on.

"A week, maybe two, a month max."

Her mouth hung open. "A month?"

"Max," he replied.

Another beep from Hanna. "All right, well, I have to go. I'm sorry. I'll call you when I get off."

"You get off at one, right? I'll already be at the airport. We might miss each other altogether." His voice already seemed so far away and distant.

"Then, if I can't get through, we'll have to talk when you land. But I have to go." She didn't wait for him to respond before she cut him off and picked up Hanna's call. "Hello?"

"Liz, it's Donovan. He's here in the ER."

"I'm on my way."

Liz disconnected the call and jumped up from her seat. She

would have to worry later about Chad and process her shock at him leaving so abruptly. She tossed her bottled water and hurried out of the breakroom. When she got into the elevator, she thought of Donovan and quickly pressed the button, her tears aching to flow.

"You don't know what's going on," she mumbled to herself. Still, it was ten o'clock at night, and it wasn't the time to normally see a child at the ER unless it was a true emergency. She had no choice but to fear the worst.

Liz jumped out of the elevator when the doors opened. She ran over to where Hanna stood at the desk, pacing back and forth. She caught Liz's look and stopped pacing for a moment.

"He just got here," Hanna started. "He's in bed two."

"Thank you!"

Liz hurried down the hall, slowing her pace only when she reached the room. She entered and spotted Victoria next to his bedside, her hand tightly grasped onto his.

"Hey, what's going on, bud?"

"I don't feel good," he said. He leaned up and then fell back down, touching his head.

"He's complaining of feeling dizzy, and his nosebleeds seem worse than they were before. Plus, he had a fever at the house."

Liz grabbed the thermometer. "Let me see." She held it to his forehead and took the temperature. "One hundred and three," she said. "Are you cold?"

He nodded, pulling himself up onto the pillow but looking weak and pale as he lost his balance and fell back.

"I'm going to go grab you a blanket."

Liz left the room and grabbed some cool washcloths. When she went back to the room, she spotted his mother standing over him, mumbling something. It broke her heart, and she looked away so her emotions wouldn't quickly take root.

"Here you go. You should start warming up soon." She laid it over him, and he pulled it up to his chin. "When did this start?"

Victoria sniffled, and Liz reached out and touched her hand. "Look at me," Liz whispered. "Everything is going to be all right."

Victoria nodded. "Things were getting better. I was relieved because he didn't seem to be having any more fevers and the pain seemed to be easing up. So, it looked promising. Then this morning, he woke up with a fever, and I tried everything to get it down, but to no avail. I would have brought him in sooner, but he was doing better."

Liz reached out and touched her arm. "This is not your fault. Dr. Wesley is here, so I'll grab him and have him come in. Just remember you have done nothing wrong."

Victoria nodded, but there wasn't any convincing her. Liz saw that etched on her face. She was uneasy and fidgeting, cautiously looking over at her son, and nervously biting on her nails. When she looked back and met Liz's stare, she gave a weak smile.

"I just have to have faith, right?"

Liz nodded. A moment later, she turned and left to grab the doctor. They had to take drastic measures; she was certain Dr. Wesley would realize that, too. As Liz entered the information into the computer system, she kept looking over to the patient room that Dr. Wesley hadn't yet exited. It would have been rude to interrupt him, but she was beginning to think he would never escape from the other patient.

When it felt like he would never get out there, he finally stepped out of the room. He looked at the patient's chart in his hand and documented something, then tossed the file into the folder. When he looked over, she walked over to him and handed him the chart.

He sighed and looked up. "I'll order a lab workup. Have them put a rush on it. Come with me."

He turned and knocked on Donovan's room. His mother replied, but it was muffled. Dr. Wesley entered the room, followed by Liz. "Hello. Sorry to see you both here again. I'm going to order some lab work. We'll have the results back tonight. You're going to be just fine, buddy." He patted his hand on Donovan's knee, and Liz shook her head.

Once they were back in the hallway, she heaved a noisy sigh. "Why'd you say that?" she asked.

"Say what?" He turned to look at her, confusion etched on his brow.

"That he'll be fine. You don't know that."

"Because childhood leukemia has a cure rate approaching ninety percent. There's every reason to be optimistic about his complete recovery."

Liz shook her head as they moved to the nurses' station. She tossed her pad of paper down on a desk and turned to him. "Maybe I'm not cut out for this, then."

"One tricky patient, and you're going to just give up like that?" He looked away from her. "Never saw you as a quitter, Elizabeth."

"I'm not a quitter."

When he looked back at her, he smirked.

"Then prove it. These are the patients who made you get

your degree. To help them through whatever ails them. Cases aren't always cut and dry, but they're always worth it. Don't give up on this little guy. I'm not."

He handed over the order with Donovan's lab work. "Tell them the sooner, the better."

Liz nodded and picked up the phone to dial the extension for the lab. After three long rings, a message came on.

"Thank you for calling the clinical laboratory. Our attendants are currently busy. If you need immediate assistance, press two to page the manager on call."

Liz dropped the phone on the receiver and hurried toward the front desk. Sophie, who was seated there, looked over in her direction. "If anyone asks, I had to run to the lab. There was no answer."

"Okay."

Sophie turned back to her next patient as Liz got on the elevator. She took the ride up to the lab department; it seemed to take longer than usual. She tapped on the side of the elevator, staring at the numbers as they slowly went up. By the time the elevator opened, she was ready to bust out of there. The floor was pitch black, except for a single row of lights that outlined both sides of the hallway.

"Creepy," Liz mumbled. She had never been up there after hours, and she would be all right if she never had to be up there again. It was too horror movie for her. She reached the lab and grabbed for the door. It was locked.

Liz frowned. She knew that using the lab after-hours was only for emergency use, but this was an emergency. Liz walked up and down the windows that looked out to the hallway. She peered through them, hoping to find someone in there. As she went back to the glass door, she spotted a note tacked onto it. *For immediate service, call the manager on call at 1-888-550-2525.*

Liz grabbed her phone from her pocket and dialed the number. It immediately went to a recording. "You've reached the lab department. Sorry, we've missed you. Leave your message, and we'll call you back."

"Uh, yeah, this is Elizabeth Fletcher, and I'm calling you because I have labs that need to be drawn for Dr. Ivan Wesley. This is an urgent matter, and I would appreciate you calling me back ASAP." She rattled off her number and then hung up.

As she waited there, not wanting to go back downstairs only to tell Dr. Wesley that she didn't know when the labs were going to be drawn. Liz tried the number again, and this time, the call clicked past the message. "You are caller number ten, and we'll be with you in a moment."

Liz frowned. It didn't make sense. Where was this call even going to? She hung up, not interested in sticking around to see if someone really would answer her after nine other people got through the line. She pulled up her contact list, and her eyes landed on Marisa's number. It wasn't right to rely on her to come through in a pinch, especially so late. *But Hanna did say that she was someone I could rely on.*

Liz hated to abuse the friendship she was building with Marisa, but she wouldn't be asking if it wasn't urgent. Who knew when someone would finally get back to her? It had to be done. Besides, it was possible that Marisa wouldn't even answer the phone.

She hit the button to call Marisa and held her breath, waiting for her to answer.

"Hello?" she answered after the second ring; Liz released her breath.

"Hey, did I wake you up? I'm sorry if I did."

"It's all right. What's going on?"

"It's Donovan. He's here at the ER, and Dr. Wesley wants labs to be done ASAP, and I can't find anyone to run the labs. I left a message with the manager on call, but I'm not sure how soon they'll call me back."

"Enter the lab orders in the computer and draw the appropriate tubes. I'll be there soon," she said.

"Are you sure? I wouldn't call and bother you, but..."

"Liz, it's fine. He needs labs done, and I'm only ten minutes from the hospital. I'll be there as soon as I can get dressed. No worries. See you in a bit."

Before Liz could voice her appreciation, Marisa hung up. It wasn't an ideal situation to have to plead with her to come to the hospital, but Liz was grateful that she at least had that backup. Now, she just had to figure out how she could express how much it meant to her.

ONE OF THE SENIOR ER NURSES WAS KIND ENOUGH TO HELP LIZ draw blood from Donovan. She lined up three pediatric tubes, each with a different color: red, blue, and purple. When the tubes were filled, Liz affixed stickers with Donovan's name, medical record number, and a bar code corresponding to the test ordered. She placed the tubes in clear plastic bags and brought them to the lab where Marisa was waiting for her.

Marisa greeted her and said, "The results will be ready in less than an hour."

Liz started to walk away but stopped. She reached out and touched Marisa's arm.

"Thank you."

Marisa looked over her shoulder and shrugged. "It's my job, Liz. No worries."

Then she was gone. Liz heaved a sigh. "God, please. He's so young. Don't take him like—"

"Elizabeth?"

She turned and looked over her shoulder at Dr. Wesley, who said, "We need to get Donovan upstairs to a room. It's going to be a long night."

"Sure thing."

Liz walked back to Donovan's room and entered. Victoria had her son cradled in her arms, his eyes droopy. "We're going to get Donovan settled into a room for the night," she said gently.

Victoria's eyes went to her. "I don't want to leave him," she said.

Liz quickly shook her head. "You don't have to leave him. They'll set you up on a cot in his room. Just gather your things and make sure you don't leave anything behind. His labs are already running and you should hear some results within the hour. I'm going to go get him set up on the children's ward."

"Thank you," his mother said.

Liz nodded and forced a smile. The prayer she was about to utter moments ago remained heavy on her mind. She had to wait to complete that, though. Liz went to the nurses' station and called up to the fourth floor.

"This is Nadine. How may I help you?"

"Hey, Nadine, it's Liz down in the ER. I have an admission

for you. His name is Donovan Prescott. Birthdate is April 12, 2015. Dr. Wesley wants him in for observation overnight while we're waiting on some results. Truthfully, he could use the rest."

"All right, I'll grab a couple of the girls to get a room around. Give us fifteen minutes before you bring him up."

"Sounds good. Thank you." Liz dropped the phone into the cradle and pressed her face into the palms of her hands. She was exhausted and, if given a chance, she would burst into tears.

"Liz?"

Liz looked up into Hanna's worried face. "You okay?"

"Not really." Liz shook her head. "Donovan is sick. I'm worried about him, Hanna. Really worried. It brings back memories of my brother all over again. How can I face that child when—"

"Shhhh." Hanna grabbed Liz's hands. "You can't think that way. I know that you're struggling. You haven't faced patients like that before, but I can assure you that if you lose faith, they'll lose faith."

"I know, but…"

"There are no buts." Hanna knelt in front of her. "Look at me."

When Liz turned her head, Hanna saw the concern etched all over her friend's face. "You've got this. Donovan will fight whatever battle he has to fight, but he's going to get through it. You got that?"

"He's going to get through it," Liz mumbled. She needed to keep saying those words. He was going to get through it because Liz would help him in whatever capacity she could.

She stood up from the chair, and Hanna joined her, wrapping her arms around her. "Thank you, Hanna."

"It's my pleasure, but eventually, you would have gotten there." She laughed, parting from the hug. "Go in there and put a smile on your face. His mother needs that."

Those were truer words than Liz could have thought herself. If she was showing despair, Victoria would quickly think the situation was worser than she needed to. She left Hanna's side and went back to the room. When she entered, Donovan's eyes were closed.

Victoria said quietly, "Donovan is the kind of kid to be so energetic. Even when he's sick, he doesn't show it. He never shows it. I know something is wrong because this isn't my little boy."

Liz wrapped her arm around Victoria. "He's in good hands, and the staff here is going to make sure that we can do everything we can for both you and him. That's why you're here, right?"

Victoria looked up and nodded. "I just never thought my child would have to go through such pain. It hurts my soul, you know?"

Liz simply nodded. "The children's ward will have a bed for him in just a few minutes. Let him sleep."

Liz reached her hand out and squeezed Victoria's. Victoria looked like she wanted to fall into a heap on the floor. Liz needed to be a rock for Donovan's mother. If she needed sleep, she wanted her to get some rest. If she needed someone to talk to, then she wanted to be that someone. This was going to be just as tough on Victoria as it was on her son.

They waited there a few minutes longer while Donovan rested in his hospital bed. When it was time, Liz looked at Victoria. "Let's go."

Liz opened the door and pushed it back against the stopper, then pushed Donovan's bed out of the room and to the elevator. She pressed the button to go up. Victoria leaned against the wall as they waited for the elevator to reach them. Finally, it did, and they loaded the bed inside.

"How long will he have to be here?" Victoria asked. "I should call my parents to let them know and see if they can get me a change of clothes. Plus, Donovan needs some stuffed animals. He needs comfort from his home." She sniffled and reached her hand up to cover her face.

Liz wasn't sure of the answer to that question, as it would all depend on the results of the lab tests. She didn't want to give false hope or give an estimate that was way off. She reached out and touched Victoria's arm as Victoria uncovered her face. Her eyes were red again.

"I'm not sure," she admitted. "We'll get the results back and then go from there."

Victoria nodded, seemingly satisfied with that answer, even if the tears were fresh on her cheeks. The door opened, and they stepped off the elevator.

"Donovan Prescott?" a woman asked, stepping out from behind her desk. Another nurse stood to the side.

Liz nodded, her work finished for the time being. She stood back and waited for them to get Donovan and his mother settled into the hospital room.

Liz waited until the nurses left his room before she went inside. Donovan had woken up and looked over to her, his smile widening. It was like he didn't even know what road he was about to head down, which was a good thing; the less he had to worry about, the better.

"I won't keep you both. I just wanted to make sure you didn't need anything before I head back to work."

Victoria stood up from her chair. "Thank you for everything."

"No need for thanks. You both take care. I'll check on you when I get a chance."

"Thanks again." Victoria hugged her, and Liz closed her eyes. Again, the tears were on the verge of falling. She bit back the lump in her throat and pulled from the hug.

"Anytime. I'll see you around. Rest well, bud."

She ruffled Donovan's hair, then was out the door. She hurried to the elevator and got on before falling back against the elevator wall, the door slowly closing her in. Liz waited for a breath before pressing the button to head back downstairs to the ER. But, as it started to go down, she quickly diverted its direction by pushing for the floor of the lab.

When she reached the floor, the doors opened. Liz cautiously moved toward the lab and opened the door. It was dark, other than a soft glow coming from the back room. She knocked on the door before barging in so that she wouldn't surprise Marisa. But Marisa wasn't there.

"Marisa?" Liz called out.

Marisa exited a small room, frowning at a piece of paper in her hand. She looked up, her face a mixture of angst and confusion. "Liz, everything is going to be fine. You'll see."

Liz covered her face as the tears flowed down. Marisa pulled her into her arms and just held her. It was what Liz needed at that moment, as she processed the news that her fears had been realized. Donovan was about to be rushed into the same life her brother had. And there was little she could do for him.

CHAPTER NINE

Marisa

L iz took another sip of her coffee as Marisa intently watched her. She wasn't certain how long they had been sitting in the breakroom. They had found themselves there after Marisa had finished telling her that Donovan's white blood cells were so elevated that it sealed their worst thoughts.

Liz wasn't in any position to continue working her shift after that. She had a strong connection with Donovan, especially with the way things had ended with her brother. So, Marisa just needed to be there for her and let her be. Liz took another sip of her coffee, then brushed a tear away from her eye. It was taking the last of her strength to keep herself upright. Despite that, she was more concerned about Marisa.

"You've spent all your time here," Liz said. "It's five in the morning. You should go home and get some sleep. What's it been? Five hours now? I'm fine."

"Six," Marisa mumbled.

"All the more reason you should get out of here."

Marisa tilted her head, then shook it, taking another sip of her coffee. "I'm good. After the third coffee, who needs sleep?"

Liz laughed, but her eyes dipped down. There was so much pain buried in her gaze. Marisa wanted to do whatever she could to take that pain from her. She couldn't explain why she had this overwhelming urge to take Liz's pain away, but she had never had this strong of a connection with anyone. Not even with her past girlfriend, and that startled her beyond belief.

"Well, I could use some sleep but can't even get my legs to carry me out of the hospital. So, imagine that." Liz tossed back her head as she took another drink.

"I'll help you. If you want to get out of here, you can come back to my place. It's probably closer anyway."

"I have to go home eventually, right?" Liz asked. She got up from her table and walked over to the trash can. She tossed the cup and then hesitated, her back still to Marisa.

"You don't have to be stubborn, Liz," Marisa said, joining her. "I know you're going through some pain. Lean on me. If that's what it takes, I have a shoulder, and you can use it."

"I'm not a weakling," Liz said, turning to her. Marisa's jaw dropped as Liz continued. "I feel like if I have to lean on someone, I'm going to crumble. I don't want to crumble."

"Liz," Marisa started, "it's not weak to have emotions. You are a strong woman. We might not know each other that well, but that much I know. I can see that. So, don't think for even a minute that I think you're weak."

"He's so little. He's Jimmy's age." Liz covered her face and sobbed as Marisa pulled her into her arms.

While Marisa had reservations about getting too close to Liz and was forcing herself to keep her distance, it wasn't the time to quarrel with herself over that matter. Liz needed someone, and if she did have a boyfriend, he wasn't there at that moment for her. This was the least Marisa could do for her. She was going to have to suck it up and be that shoulder for Liz. It was the mature thing to do.

"Let's get you home to my place," Marisa whispered. "You have to get some sleep. Doctor's orders."

Liz opened her mouth, but Marisa wouldn't let her argue. "If you get ill, who's that going to help?"

Liz didn't object after that. Marisa helped her out of the breakroom, and they left the hospital. She motioned toward her car, and they quietly headed in that direction.

"My car," Liz argued, but only once.

"It will wait until you've gotten your rest."

Marisa unlocked the door, and the two of them got in. They were headed to her house in less than two minutes. As she pulled out of the parking lot, she glanced over to Liz. She was already asleep, or at least her eyes were closed. Marisa turned back to the road and tried not to make any sudden movements as she didn't want to jerk Liz awake.

When she turned into the driveway and parked, she considered not bothering to wake Liz up, but the car wasn't as comfortable as the bed would be, so she reached over and gently jerked her awake.

"We're here," Marisa whispered.

Liz moaned and rubbed her eyes, pulling herself up in the seat and looking over to Marisa. "I should have just taken my car home."

Marisa smirked. "You were out cold before I even got out of the parking lot. Doubt you would have made it." She motioned with her head toward the door. "Come on. You need to get some good rest."

Liz eventually reached for the door and got out of the car. They walked to the entrance, with Liz lagging at least two feet behind Marisa. Marisa unlocked the door and held it open for Liz to enter.

"I'll grab you something to wear to sleep in," Marisa began.

"Not necessary. I can sleep in my scrubs, and I'll take the couch. I'm easy."

Marisa rolled her eyes. "You'll recall I said you needed *good* rest, not adequate rest. Again, you don't need to be so stubborn. You're here, so just let me help you to relax."

Liz nodded, and Marisa led the way down a hallway. She stopped at her bedroom and went in to find lounge pants and a T-shirt. She brought them out to Liz and led the way to the spare bedroom.

"Make yourself comfortable and don't wake up until you're ready."

"What about your work?" Liz asked.

"I'm off, as are you. I've already checked the schedule, so get some rest."

Liz nodded, and Marisa slowly backed out of the bedroom. Liz was uncomfortable allowing Marisa to help her out, as she was clearly an independent woman, but Marisa was relieved Liz was finally allowing the help and hoped that she didn't wake for at least three hours. Marisa escaped into her room, ready to fall into bed, the coffee slowly wearing off. She collapsed into bed, but her mind went to the woman down the hall. Liz was so close, in the same house. Thinking about that too much would drive her nuts, so she focused on her breath and let sleep take her.

Liz's body was warm against hers as Marisa pulled Liz closer to her. Liz's breath was warm, too, just as their lips touched. Marisa felt Liz's tongue slowly invading her mouth, and she gasped, grabbing hold of Liz's arms, then trailing her hands down Liz's bare back until the agony of her being so close yet so far away from her came crashing down upon her.

"I need you," Liz whispered, those words echoing throughout Marisa's brain. Was she really hearing those words from the woman who made her body tingle, the woman Marisa was left craving?

Marisa heard those words again.

"I need you, Marisa."

It sounded even better with her name.

She had longed to hear that from Liz. Her heart pounded wildly in her chest as Liz's sweet and innocent body—filled with youth yet so much maturity—caressed hers.

"I need you, too," Marisa groaned. She needed her more than she needed air to breathe.

Just as their lips collided, Marisa's chest caved in. She gasped for air and jolted up, her breathing raspy. When she stared ahead at her empty bed, she felt dread. She was alone.

"Ugh!" she groaned, falling back into her bed and staring up, her eyes darting around the dots that were scattered unevenly across the length and width of the ceiling.

Liz came back into her memory, but not the Liz from the dream that had invaded her sleep. That was hot and sexy, and she desperately wanted to get back to it, but the thoughts she had now were the thoughts of earlier and the struggle Liz was going through.

"Liz!"

Marisa looked at her alarm clock and covered her face. Was it really that late?

Still fully dressed, she jumped out of bed and hurried out of the room, down the hallway to Liz's bedroom. She peeked into the room and she saw that the bed was made and Liz was gone. She hurried back the other way and rounded the corner. She hesitated when she saw Liz standing at the mantle. She had a picture in her hand.

"Who's the woman?" Liz asked.

Marisa entered the room. "My ex," she said. She reached out and grabbed the picture from her. "Guess I haven't gotten around to cleaning my mantle."

She looked down at the picture. It'd been a while since she was able to look at it and not get a pang of regret in her chest—regret that her life didn't work out the way she had wanted it to. But, at that moment, she didn't feel anything but pride at the thought of how far she had come. She laid the picture facedown on the table and looked at Liz. "It was a long time ago."

"Ex," Liz said softly as if turning it over in her mind and making the connection. Now, there was no more hiding that Marisa was a lesbian.

"How long?" Liz asked.

"About a year. Too long to keep the picture hanging around?"

"Well, that depends," Liz started. "Are you still holding out hope that she's coming back?"

"No. That's long past. She's moved on." Marisa shrugged. "And so have I."

Liz looked over to the picture, and Marisa cringed. "I know how this looks, but honestly, I rarely have time to spend in the living room. Maybe I should have cleared away that picture long ago, but it doesn't mean I still feel anything for her. I'm just a lazy housekeeper."

She laughed, hoping to lighten the mood. Liz did get a slight smile on her lips over that comment.

"Enough about me, though. What about you? How are you feeling? Did you get enough sleep? I didn't realize it was so late. Apparently, I needed rest, too."

"Got a couple of hours in. It was much needed. Feeling a little better. I didn't want to wake you. There was a laundry basket, and I dropped your pajamas in there. Hope that was all right."

"Yeah, that's fine. Thanks."

Liz nodded. "I had considered getting an Uber back to my car, but then found myself in the living room."

"Looking at my pictures," Marisa teased. Liz's eyes widened, and Marisa waved her hand in front of her. "I'm only teasing. There's nothing off-limits here. But I imagine you're hungry. I know I'm famished. Do you like eggs? I could make breakfast."

She glanced at her watch and laughed. "Er, brunch," she amended, leading the way to the kitchen.

"That's really not necessary," Liz argued, coming up from behind her. "If anything, I would owe you breakfast. I could buy you something on the way back to my car. Or we could grab something at the cafeteria."

Marisa opened the refrigerator. "Or, you can help me whip us up something. No point in spending money when I have a kitchen full of food."

She looked over her shoulder, and Liz threw up her hands. "Grab a bowl from the cupboard." She pointed, and Liz obeyed.

Marisa smiled as they worked on making eggs and bacon, and even pancakes. It was good to have someone else in the kitchen, helping to do the work and even offering up some good conversation. Cooking helped her to keep her mind off the dream that had woken her up. The more she moved around, the more she was certain she could leave that dream behind her. But the minute she stopped and looked Liz's way, the dream came rushing back to her, causing her cheeks to get red.

Marisa slowly released a breath and pushed on. She flipped the pancakes in the skillet. Liz stood directly behind her, and she felt her eyes on her. "Did you minor in cooking?"

Marisa laughed loudly. "Not hardly. You know what my minor was?"

She placed the skillet back on the stove and turned to look at her. Liz tilted her head, her eyes wide.

"Dancing." She shook her head. "Looking back, I wonder why I went with something like that. I mean, it's not like I'll get any use from it. But then again, that was a long time ago." Marisa turned back to the stove and continued working on the food in front of her.

Liz stepped up next to her and stirred the eggs. Her arm

touched Liz's, and Marisa quickly stepped to the side. If Liz got too close, Marisa was liable to give away all her secrets, and Liz would see that she was sexually appealing to her.

"We'll have to go dancing sometime, and you can show me what you've learned," Liz said.

Marisa turned her head to look at Liz, who was still focused on the eggs and bacon in front of her. "We could, but I doubt I remember anything."

She also doubted getting Liz on the dance floor was a smart move. Marisa glanced at the pancakes and picked them up, flipping them once more. "Looks like we're done," Marisa said.

They pulled the food from the stove and put it on the placemats on the counter, then Marisa grabbed the plates from the cupboard and dished the food out while Liz grabbed the butter and syrup from the refrigerator. It was definitely a unique situation they had been tossed into, but it made things even more difficult for Marisa as she was struggling to get that dream out of her mind while having the real thing in her kitchen at the same time.

They sat down and ate, and the conversation stagnated. Liz focused on her food as she took each bite, and Marisa tried to keep her eyes off the woman across the table from her.

Suddenly, Liz snapped her head up. "Hey," she said, reaching across the table to touch Marisa's forearm. "I'm not sure how to fully express my gratitude because you've done so much for me lately. You've given me comfort when I've been a mess and you came to the hospital last night to help. You even let me stay here when I was too tired and emotional to get myself home. It means a lot to me. Thank you for everything,

Marisa. I needed you and you came without a second thought. That means so much to me."

As she squeezed Marisa's arm tenderly, Marisa's heart slammed against her chest. She thought of leaning forward and kissing Liz, giving in to her feelings. No one had ever shown such gratitude to her before or recognized her efforts like this.

She shoved a bite of food into her mouth, pulling away from Liz's touch before she did something she shouldn't. She couldn't cross that line. Ever. "You're very sweet," she said. "I'm happy I could help, and you're very welcome."

Liz perked up with more energy than she had shown in a while. The rest must have really helped to recharge her. "What do you like most? Brownies? Cookies?"

Marisa laughed. "Why do you ask?"

"I want to bake you something to show my appreciation. Brownies?"

"You don't need to do that. But, sure. Brownies."

They smiled at each other until Marisa broke eye contact and chugged water. She probably needed to ask Liz to leave soon before anything happened.

The pep in Liz's posture faded and her shoulders drooped. "I wonder what he's doing right now."

"I imagine they're running him through some tests. He's probably nervous, but his mother seems to be a strong influence in his life. He's lucky to have her."

As Liz looked up, Marissa saw there were tears back in her eyes. "He's lucky to have you, too, a nurse who cares a great deal about him."

"I'm sure everyone thinks I care too much. Like, what kind

of fruit loop am I?" She shook her head and dropped her fork into her dish.

"You're not a fruit loop." Liz met her gaze, and Marisa continued. "Can I let you in on a secret?"

Liz nodded.

"I've never told anyone this before, but when I first decided to become a laboratory technician and got this job, I thought I was invincible. I thought that if I saw sick people, it wouldn't affect me. I thought I had the backbone and nothing would phase me. The first week I was at the hospital was the first week I realized how wrong I was. I was working in a lab, and a patient came in. She was about thirteen years old. She had labs just like Donovan did. It was a routine checkup. She was seeing a new doctor, and they wanted to run routine blood tests. No biggie. But then things fell apart. It turns out she had brain cancer, and without the lab work, they would have never caught it.

"I watched her for a year of her life struggling and in so much pain, and she was alone. She was a foster child. She was abandoned when she was two and left in the system, and she was fostered out to this family, but the minute she got the brain cancer diagnosis, she was abandoned again. They said they couldn't afford her medical care. I don't know their situation, and maybe that was the case, but I know there are government benefits as a foster parent, and I was angry. Angry that they were leaving this little girl to suffer alone.

"But she was strong. She had the most beautiful spirit, and she didn't let that get to her. While I was angry, she was fighting for her life and still smiling through it all. So as time went on, I had to continue doing regular blood tests on her, and I saw her gradually getting sicker all while being in the foster care system, which, don't even get me started on that…"

Marisa shuddered just thinking about it. "She was alone. So, I attempted to foster her, and the paperwork was going through, but before it was finalized, she took a turn for the worse. We never got it finalized because she wound up passing away—in my arms. And at that moment, I wanted to give up. I didn't think this job was for me, either."

Liz gasped. "Wow…"

Marisa nodded, looking down at her nearly empty plate. "We have more in common than you may ever know. I saw someone I loved dearly die in front of me, and your brother…" Marisa looked up, reaching Liz's gaze, which once again was full of tears. "It might not be the same thing. She wasn't my family, but she sure felt like it."

Liz nodded slowly. "It was the same thing."

Marisa took a bite of her pancake, then slowly ate through it. Liz wiped her tears away.

Marisa considered her nagging thoughts, then sighed. "So, you saw a picture of my past, but what about you? Any significant other? Boyfriend in the picture?"

Marisa braced herself, wanting to know the truth once and for all. If what Hanna had said was true, Marisa needed to keep Liz at arm's length away, even if it was a struggle. It would be easier than getting too close only to get her heart broken even deeper.

Liz stirred her fork in her plate of eggs. "Yeah, but it's complicated. There's someone, but I'm not sure how strong that connection is anymore."

Marisa bit back the smile. So, while there was a man out

there, it didn't seem like Liz was too set on him. That was a good sign, even if Marisa didn't know why she cared so much. So what if this woman who was technically young enough to be her daughter was possibly on the market? She wasn't prepared to be with a woman like that, and she needed to have her brain examined if she felt otherwise. It was best just to push those sexual images clear from her mind because it wasn't happening.

CHAPTER TEN

Liz

Making her way up to Donovan's room was harder than Liz expected. As the doors opened, she considered going straight back down. It had been two days since she had first left him in the children's ward. She was nervous to see him and determine how things were going based on the doctors' projections.

When she reached his room, she released a slow and steady breath. "You've got this," she whispered.

She entered his room and halted when she saw that the sign was cleared of his name; plus, the bed was empty. Liz backed out of the room and went to the nurses' desk. Nadine sat there, staring at her computer.

"Hey, Nadine. I know it's been a couple of days, but where's Donovan?"

She looked up, confused. "Didn't you hear?"

Liz's mouth went dry, and she stared at her. That was never a good thing to hear, especially if you feared bad news. "Hear what?"

"Oh. Nothing like that. Your face just went three shades whiter." She laughed and stood up, then pointed down the hallway. "He was transferred to the oncology service."

Liz released a sigh, feeling the weight that had plummeted in her stomach. "Thank you!"

She hadn't considered they would move him. It made perfect sense, but she was a little frustrated she hadn't heard the news. It would have saved her some heartache. Still, it was better than having to hear the alternative. She walked down the hallway and moved on to the next section. She came to another desk, where a woman whom she didn't recognize sat. Upon a closer glance, she saw the volunteer tag attached to her badge.

"Hi, may I help you?" the woman asked.

"Hi, Crystal. I'm Liz. I work in the ER, and there's a patient up here I was working with and just wanted to follow up on. I don't know if you can give me that access…"

"Sure thing. What's the name?"

"Donovan Prescott."

Crystal looked down at the computer and clicked around, just like someone like Nadine would normally do. Liz had no idea that they had volunteers who could come in and have so much control over what was happening around the hospital.

She looked up and pointed to the door behind Liz. "He's right in there."

"Great! Thank you!"

Liz turned and went to the door. She softly knocked before

letting herself in. Victoria was at Donovan's bed, reading him a story, and they both looked over to her as she entered the room.

"Liz!" Donovan cried, jumping up.

"Be careful," Victoria ordered. She jumped up to grab him by the waist.

Liz smiled as she moved closer to bed. "Hey, kiddo." He threw his arms around her neck, already standing on top of the bed. "How are you doing?"

"Good!" he said.

When Liz looked at Victoria, she saw that Victoria had a smile on her face, but her eyes seemed dim and dark. Liz helped Donovan back into the bed, then sat on the corner of his bed. His grin hadn't once faded.

"Just wanted to stop in on my break to see how things were going. I didn't realize you had been moved. When did that happen?"

"Yesterday afternoon," Victoria said. "They wanted to provide him more care."

"Well, that's not all that bad of an idea," Liz added. "You look good, though." Liz tossed a look to Victoria. "He does, doesn't he?"

Victoria's eyes grew wider, and she nodded. "He's doing well."

"Mom was just reading me a new book she bought." He grabbed the book and held it out to her.

"Can't buy a whole lot at the gift shop." Victoria laughed and then looked up at Liz.

Liz saw a cover with a boy in a bed, a bandage around his head, and a basic title. *Scotty Goes to the Hospital.*

"Maybe I can read it sometime," Liz said, smiling as she

handed the book back to Victoria. "Are the doctors treating you well?"

"I really like Mindi," he said.

"She's the nurse who's handling his care," Victoria explained when Liz shot a questioning look toward her.

"As much as you like me?" Liz teased.

Donovan giggled. "No, silly."

Liz beamed and put her hand against his forehead. He felt nice and cool, so that was good. She dropped her hand and brushed it against his pillow.

"I'll leave you two to catch up," Victoria said, getting up from the spot next to the bed.

"You don't have to go," Liz argued.

She shook her head. "I think this is good for him. I'll be back."

Liz turned back to Donovan. "Are you comfortable?" she asked.

He nodded. "A little hungry, maybe." He touched his stomach, and it growled, making Liz laugh.

"Give me a sec." She held up a finger and quickly left his room. Crystal remained at the front desk. "Is there anywhere here where I can get pudding or something? Donovan's a tad hungry."

"We have a fruit cup." She reached under the desk and pulled it from a refrigerator, then handed Liz a spoon.

"Thanks!"

Liz went back into his room, holding the cup up like a trophy. He beamed brighter. "Do you like fruit?"

"Love it!"

He reached out for it, grabbed it from her hands, and then

tried to get the lid off. He groaned, which brought a smile to Liz's lips.

"Allow me."

She removed the lid and handed the cup back to him. Donovan eagerly dug into it. After a few bites, he looked up. "What's that smirk for?" Liz asked, taking her seat.

"You know what this reminds me of?" he asked.

"Let me see…" She tapped her mouth as if in thought. "When we first met? Taking you out to have some Jell-O?"

He nodded. "You got it."

He took another couple of bites, and Liz just relaxed in the chair, watching him. It was good seeing him smile. She feared that she'd enter the room and find him hooked up to machines or something. But he hadn't started treatment yet. That would probably come several days later after they had all their testing in.

And Marisa had helped so much. Even now while she spent time with Donovan, Liz couldn't stop thinking about how Marisa had been there when she most needed her. It had felt a little odd sleeping at her house but also thrilling. It had given her an even stronger sense of who Marisa was and brought their relationship out into the real world. Liz never imagined that she could feel so comfortable around someone, so important and listened to. She definitely never felt that way around Chad, and he would never drop everything to come be with her.

A knot formed in her stomach. He had sent her a message to say he had landed safely in France, but she hadn't responded to his messages much since. Work was constantly draining her, but she also didn't feel any spark between them. He rarely asked how she was and mostly just talked about everything he was experiencing in France. Part of her felt relieved that she didn't need to put on a fake smile for dates or pretend like everything was okay since he never wanted to talk about anything heavy. The other part of her felt guilty for not being more responsive or missing him.

With Marisa, she was free to be herself. She could express her emotions and get the support she craved. And learning that Marisa was into women had changed everything.

But that was a silly thought. She liked Marisa as a coworker and friend. She did find her attractive, but she was a woman. She was also a lot older. Liz had no idea what a romantic relationship with an older woman would be like.

Besides, she doubted Marisa would even be interested in someone like her—an emotional wreck.

"Will I ever get to go outside again?" Donovan asked, pulling Liz back into the moment.

Liz looked up and made eye contact. "Of course you will."

That question hurt Liz—to even think he would ask something like that. No kid should need to worry about something like seeing the sun again.

"I'll tell you what. If the weather is nice and you're feeling up to it, sometime within the next week, I'll come back here and take you out to the garden. It's beautiful out there. Just you and me. Deal?"

He nodded. "I like that."

There was a knock on the door, and Liz turned to see a nurse coming into the room. "Hey, I'm Mindi," she said.

"Liz. I work in the ER."

Mindi's eyes lit up. "I've heard a lot about you. This little guy can't stop talking about the nurse before me." She grinned. "I have to run my vitals. It shouldn't take too long."

"Hey, bud. I have to get back to work." Liz leaned in and kissed Donovan's forehead. "I'll be back in a few days."

"Bye, Liz!" Donovan called out.

Liz waved and then left his room. Victoria stood against the wall, her eyes closed. Liz approached her cautiously. "How are you doing?"

Victoria opened her eyes and nodded. "Pretty well, all things considering. He meets with the specialist tomorrow morning, so we'll have a better understanding of what's going on."

"I'll be praying," Liz said. "I mean, I've been praying. But I will continue to."

She smiled. "Thank you! He needs all the prayers possible. He really likes you."

"Your boy is darling. I told him if he's feeling up to it and you're okay with it, I'll come and take him outside. There's a garden on the south side that's breathtaking. I think it could lift his spirits."

"That would be awesome. He would love that and, frankly, it would be nice to have a short break. Never knew just sitting and lying around could be so exhausting."

Liz smiled and reached out to stroke her arm. "He's going to be all right. I have faith that you'll get through this rough patch, and it'll be behind you when he's in remission."

Victoria nodded and then looked past her to Donovan's room. Liz turned as Mindi exited. "I have to get back to work. But I'll be back in a few days."

"Thank you!" Victoria hugged her and then went back inside as Liz headed over to Mindi.

"Can I talk to you for a minute?"

"Sure!" Mindi turned to her.

"How do I go about volunteering on this floor?"

Mindi frowned. "Volunteering? You're a nurse, and surely that leaves you rather busy, especially in the ER. I've heard horror stories. How would you have time?"

Liz shrugged. "Just a couple of days a week. It wouldn't have to be much. I feel compelled to do this, but is it an option?"

She smirked. "This floor could use all the volunteers it can get. There's always a shortage. I'll let my boss know. I'm sure he'll be in touch."

"Great! Thanks!"

Liz left Mindi, feeling better about everything, knowing that Donovan was in good hands and being glad to be a part of it. It was something she felt compelled to do. She loved kids and looked forward to being able to help them instead of looking in from the outside. It was an opportunity she couldn't ignore.

LIZ SUNK INTO THE SEAT ACROSS FROM HER COMPUTER. IT HAD been a long day, and she was ready for it to end, but her shift wasn't over. "Three more hours," she groaned, rubbing her face.

"Wanna go to break?" Sally asked as she popped up at the desk.

Liz jumped. "Didn't see you there."

"I tend to be stealth-like." Sally grinned, plopping down in the seat next to her. "But I saw you zoned out looking at the computer. Thought maybe you were ready for a break."

"Sure!" Liz stood to her feet as the phone rang. "I'll be back in fifteen."

Before she could step around, Sally was already motioning her back.

"Call for you."

Liz frowned, grabbing the phone from her. "Hello?"

"Liz? This is Mindi, Donovan's nurse."

The blood rushed from Liz's face. "Yeah, I remember. Is Donovan all right?"

"Oh, yes. No worries about Donovan. He's hanging in there. He just had his first chemo treatment yesterday, so there are some things he's dealing with, but that's not why I'm calling. My boss, Trace, asked me to give you a call. He has a few minutes this afternoon and wanted to sit down with you. I told him you're interested in working as a volunteer on this floor. If you have a few minutes within the next hour, he would like to chat with you."

"Oh. Okay. I'm working currently, but…" She held the phone away from her ear. "Can you handle the afternoon for a bit? They want to see me upstairs in the children's ward. Shouldn't be long."

Sally shrugged. "Not going anywhere, so sure."

She went back to her call. "Thirty minutes?"

"Sounds good. I'll let him know. We'll see you then." Mindi's cheery voice came through the phone, and then the call was dropped.

Liz placed the phone back into the receiver and considered the conversation. On a whim, she had considered volunteer work, but she was now looking forward to getting up there and seeing what Trace had to say.

"Are you sure you can handle it? This morning has been kind of busy. I don't want to put added stress on you."

"Don't even think about it. I'm fine. Hanna comes in an hour, right?"

Liz checked her watch and nodded. "I'll be back, then. See ya!"

She waved and then went to the elevator to first take her break. As she got off the elevator, her phone rang without fail. Every time she was on the verge of getting a few minutes alone, Chad called or messaged. She felt like maybe he had a camera on her and knew when she was free to chat. She slipped the phone back into her pocket. And just like many other times, Liz ignored the call, trying not to linger on her guilt.

He and I really need to talk about this whole engagement thing. I think we rushed into it.

Chad probably wanted to go on and on about his experiences, so why damper her mood when she would be going straight into a conversation with Trace after her break? Ignoring the call, sadly, seemed like the only option to take.

When she opened the door to the breakroom, she went straight to the refrigerator and pulled out her iced coffee. She sighed, taking a drink. *Perfect!* She turned to walk to a table when she saw Marisa with her head buried in her phone.

Liz smirked. Their paths always seemed to cross. But Liz didn't mind. Despite her confusion about what she felt for Marisa—if it was really more than friendship—there was something about Marisa's presence that made the world feel okay again. She also gave really great hugs.

"Reading something interesting?" Liz asked, taking the seat

across from her. When Marisa looked up, she pushed her phone away, then shrugged. "Oh? Not interesting, then?"

Marisa laughed. "You might call it lame."

"Try me." Liz took a drink of her coffee.

"*Lab Weekly*. New articles drop every Monday."

"And yet, today is Wednesday." Liz scrunched up her nose. A soft chuckle came from across the table.

"Sometimes I like to read the articles over again. Get more knowledge that way." Marisa shrugged. "Told you. Lame. But hey, that's where my old person's mind goes." She picked up her cup and took a drink of whatever she had.

"Not my idea of fun," Liz admitted. "But I wouldn't ever call you lame. We all have our preferences."

Liz put her bottle down and reached for Marisa's phone. "Let's see what this is all about." She made a face. "Coagulation and blood clotting? Intriguing."

Marisa rolled her eyes. "How thrilling!"

Liz shook her head and took another sip of her coffee. "So, did you get my brownies?"

"No. What do you mean?"

"Well, I baked brownies to show my appreciation for every-thing you've done and I left them in the lab for you. Samantha was there when I dropped them off and said you'd be in soon. You didn't get them?"

Marisa frowned. "No. How strange."

"Bummer. I also baked some for Hanna and the other nurses since they've been so patient with me. They all loved them. Well, I'll bake you another batch." Switching subjects, she added, "But I have news. You might not find this all that exciting either." Liz crossed her legs and stared across the table at Marisa.

"Oh yeah? What's that?" Marisa arched an eyebrow and didn't respond further as Liz told her about the volunteering opportunity.

"Just thinking that it's what I need. It will make me feel like I'm doing something to make a change."

Liz beamed, waiting to hear what Marisa felt about that, but Marisa remained quiet. She looked like she was about to open her mouth, but she didn't respond.

"You have nothing to say?"

Marisa tilted her head in response.

"Come on, Marisa. There's something you want to say. Are you afraid that it will upset me? Or maybe you think I'll tell you to mind your own business?"

Marisa laughed. "Are you going to get all high and mighty and respond as such?"

"No, but I can sense that you have something to say, and there has to be a reason you won't come out with it."

Marisa sighed. "I'm not afraid to say something," she began. "Maybe I'm apprehensive, I guess." She shrugged. "Not my call, really. That's on you. If this is what you want to do, then go for it."

Liz's phone rang, and she pulled it from her pocket. Chad's name flashed on the screen again. She quickly pushed it back into her pocket and looked back at Marisa. "I guess I thought you might not find it interesting but would at least be excited for me. You're kind of disappointing me here."

She looked away, then back to Marisa. "Why aren't you excited?"

"It's not that I'm not excited for you. If this is what you want to do, then I think that's great."

"You just don't approve. Maybe even wondering why I would want to do this? Think I'm biting off too much?"

Marisa pointed with her finger. "That's one thing I question. But then, am I wrong, or were you close to calling quits on this profession? You even thought you couldn't handle it. I saw the struggle you felt with one kid. Yet, you're now throwing yourself into the fire? What if you get attached to other patients who just don't make it?"

"That's true," Liz muttered, looking down at her drink and wondering if she could fully throw herself into the flames of working the children's cancer ward and what that would entail. "I like children, and I want to be a force of a good. It's only a volunteer position. You know, two or three days. And if it gets to be too much, I'll pull back."

"Guess maybe I want to be the level-headed voice of reason here. I worry that you're getting in too deep. You can't get attached to all these children and watch the pain they're going through. Remember? I know that."

Marisa was trying to be a mother to her about it, and while Liz wanted to appreciate her thoughts on the matter, it was tough hearing that Marisa didn't think she was prepared for the volunteer position.

Marisa stood up and grabbed her phone, pocketing it. "I have to go back to work, but if you're sure that this is something you want to do, then I trust that you've considered it fully. If you have, then sounds good. See you around."

She left the table, and Liz let those words sink in. She tended to jump into things blindly, and this was one thing she had jumped headfirst into. But the thought of being there for Donovan and all the other kids made her happy. She would be just fine with that.

Her phone rang for the third time. Again, Chad's name flashed on the screen. This time she turned the phone off so he couldn't interrupt her any further. She left the breakroom and went up to the floor where she was to meet with Trace. She saw Mindi at the front desk, so she walked over to her.

"Liz," she began. "He's down the hall and last door on the right. He's waiting for you."

As Liz walked toward Trace's office, she caught a glimpse of Donovan's door, which was tightly closed. Usually, they left it open or ajar. She pushed away any frantic thoughts she had and proceeded to where Trace was. She knocked on the door and waited for his greeting.

"Come in!"

She opened the door and stepped in, ready to impress him. He greeted her with a handshake. "Elizabeth Fletcher, I presume?"

Liz nodded.

"The name is Trace Reece. Have a seat and tell me why you want to volunteer on this floor."

There it was, the question she had to face before she would be able to get the job. A million thoughts went through her mind, but she had to focus on the one thing that was her truth and not think about what Marisa thought about it. She was doing what was best for her, even if she did feel some doubt about it.

CHAPTER ELEVEN

Marisa

A knock on the door signaled Marisa to look up. Samantha entered the lab and collapsed against the wall. "Hey there. The last patient signed out."

"Yes, thankfully," Samantha replied. "So, I was wondering what you were doing tonight."

Marisa shrugged. "Busy night ahead of me. More Netflix. More wine." She laughed. "You?"

"Well, that's kind of why I'm in here."

Marisa continued to look down at her paperwork, not realizing Samantha was moving closer to her.

"You see, my sister is the only one home, and I'm sure her jerk of a boyfriend will be there. They'll be hooking up to try to move this baby along further."

Marisa looked up as Samantha continued, "That's a whole

other story. Anyway, I'm not looking forward to the sounds that will come from them as they're, well, you know…" Her eyes dropped, and Marisa smirked.

"Pretty sure I know. So, would you like to come over?"

Samantha looked up, and her smile deepened as she nodded. "Please."

"Let me finish up here. Give me ten minutes, and I'll be out."

"Thank you!"

"Oh, by the way, did Liz come by the other day to drop off brownies?"

With a poker face, Samantha said, "No. Why?"

"No reason."

As Samantha spun on her heel and went back out to her computer, Marisa frowned. She believed Liz, so why would Samantha lie about something like that?

Dismissing it for now, she turned back to her computer and stared at it for a moment until she pushed her work to the side. It could wait until the next day when she had a clearer mind.

"Are you ready to go?" Marisa asked, throwing her purse over her shoulder.

"That was fast," Samantha said, jumping up from her desk.

"Decided work could wait. I just had paperwork to do anyway. Turn the lights off on your way out, and let's get out of here."

Marisa was ready to dig into a bottle of wine. As she left the hospital, her mind wandered back to Liz. She was most likely gone for the evening. The way things had strayed for them was awkward because she got the feeling that she had said something wrong, at least in Liz's eyes. Liz wanted to hear what she wanted to hear, but that wasn't Marisa's job. Marisa wasn't supposed to tell Liz what would make her feel better. That was the immaturity in Liz, and it came with her age.

It was Marisa's job to be honest with her. And in her honest opinion, Liz wasn't someone who could go running into the fire for a bunch of kids who were in desperate need of help. If she couldn't handle one child having to struggle, how could she handle twenty and all at the same time? Marisa was only thinking about Liz and what would benefit her. She wanted to be wrong, but at that moment, she didn't think she was.

"Do you want to follow me?" Marisa asked.

"Sure! I'm parked right over there." Samantha pointed to a small gray SUV. Marisa got into her car and watched as Samantha got out and pulled out of her parking spot. Samantha drove over to her, giving Marisa enough room to get out of her spot.

One good thing about Samantha going to the house with her was she wouldn't have to face the house alone. As many people have said in the past, it was probably lonely, and that was true. Marisa was caught with the loneliness way too often. She thought she had gotten over that and was dealing with her loneliness just fine, but having Liz stay with her the other night brought all that sadness back to the surface. She needed the company tonight. It didn't have to be a sexual connection, just someone she could talk with so she wouldn't have to be stuck alone with her thoughts running wild.

Marisa turned into the driveway and parked, then got out of the car and waited for Samantha to get there. When Samantha parked and got out of her car, Marisa asked, "White or red wine?"

"You choose. I'm not picky."

Marisa pointed to the living room. "Have a seat. I'll be out in a minute." Marisa grabbed two glasses and a bottle of white wine and then carried them out to Samantha. She poured her a glass, then handed it over. "Enjoy!" she said. "Any preferences as to what we watch?"

Marisa turned on the television and took a sip of her wine, waiting for Samantha to give her suggestions.

"So, you'll think I'm totally weird," Samantha started, "but I'm in love with those reality-type dating shows."

Marisa raised an eyebrow, and Samantha took another sip. "Told you you'd think I was weird."

"Weird is such a strong word," Marisa said. "But I've learned a lot about you recently. You read Harry Potter and love reality dating shows. Are you sure you're twenty-one?"

"Twenty-two, actually. Today's my birthday."

"What?" Marisa jumped up from the couch. "Why didn't you say something? The office could have served up some cake or something. Hold that thought."

She left the living room and went into the kitchen. She opened her cupboard and reached into a box, pulling out a Twinkie. Having known Samantha for three years, she felt bad that she didn't know when her birthday was, but they didn't always have time to talk during work, and that wasn't the type of thing they discussed at the hospital. Still, it bothered her that she was finding out at the last minute, especially when Samantha was sitting on her couch.

"It's not a birthday cake, but it will have to do." She tossed the wrapped Twinkie to Samantha.

Samantha laughed and held it up. "Thank you!"

"My pleasure, but I'm confused right now." Marisa turned off the television. "Why are you here and not out with some guy or something? Or you could be with your parents. Doesn't make sense to me."

Samantha shrugged, taking a bite of her Twinkie. "My parents had plans, and as you've heard, I'm struggling with who I want to date. So, I guess it just helped that you offered up your place for me to hang out."

"You should have told me it was your birthday, but happy to have you." Marisa took a drink of her wine. "And, since it's your birthday, you'll definitely get your choice of shows. So, reality TV it is." She made a face, and Samantha snickered.

"You'll love it."

Marisa wasn't certain that she would. She had lost all interest in reality TV just the first year that that one show set on an island came out. Getting back into it wasn't her idea of entertainment, but she had to just give it a try for Samantha's sake. She turned the TV back on, started the show that Samantha pointed to, and tried to just focus on her wine.

Samantha jumped up and turned the lights off. "That's better."

"It's not a movie," Marisa teased.

Samantha plopped down on the couch next to her, and even in the dark, Marisa saw her smiling. If she thought about it, it seemed like that was the first real smile she had seen from Samantha in months. To happen on her birthday—all the better.

But as the show went on, Samantha got into it way more than anyone should. She was beaming over the men and women as if she had some sort of stake in whether they made a relation-ship work. Marisa couldn't help but laugh.

Two episodes in, Marisa had poured herself a second glass of wine, but Samantha had barely touched her first glass. Another two episodes passed, and Marisa stared at her fourth glass and shook her head. If she had any more, she would find herself passed out on the couch. She got up and left the living room to go to the kitchen.

She poured coffee into the maker and leaned against the counter, just watching the coffee maker percolating in front of her. That was more entertaining than the show they were binging in the living room. She glanced at her watch. It was already two o'clock. She would never throw Samantha out of the house, but she did wonder how much longer Samantha would want to watch TV. That was nothing, though, and defi-nitely not reality.

"You don't much care for the show."

Marisa glanced over her shoulder as Samantha entered the kitchen, her glass in her hand. She took a long drink, then made a face. "Flat."

"It's been sitting for four hours," Marisa replied with a laugh. She grabbed the glass. "Coffee is on. As for the show, it's not all that convincing. Do relationships really work out of these?"

"A few," she replied. "Guess it helps to get my mind off my relationships." She leaned back against the wall, and Marisa stared at her. "It can be entertaining if you get swept up in the characters."

Marisa pointed to her. "You just called them characters. But it's real life, right?"

The coffee timer went off, and Marisa turned to pour them both cups. She handed one over to Samantha, then took a seat at the table.

"When I say characters, I just mean everyone has characteristic traits that come out." Samantha moved to the chair across from Marisa. "I know that it's not necessarily the type of show everyone likes. Me, I would watch all the new ones with my mom as I was growing up. It was kind of our thing. Now that she's gotten older, she doesn't much care for it either."

Samantha took a sip of the coffee as Marisa took one of her own. She winced as the hot coffee touched her tongue. "It happens when you get older, I suppose. Your likes tend to differ from years past."

"So, can I ask you something?" Samantha asked.

"Depends," Marisa teased. "I'm kidding. Of course."

"What type are you really attracted to? What are some deal breakers of yours? What are your turn-ons and turn-offs?"

"Geesh, that's more than just one question." Marisa took a drink of her coffee, giving herself time to consider her answers. Why Samantha wanted to ask these questions was beyond Marisa, but no question was off-limits for her. If Samantha wanted to know, then Marisa would answer.

"I'm inquisitive. What can I say?" Samantha shrugged.

"Does it have something to do with your own relationships, wanting advice and all? You never did tell me who you're crushing on at work. My money is still on Alan."

Samantha sat there for a moment and stared down into her coffee. Marisa felt like that long silence gave her the answer she expected. After a moment, Samantha looked up, avoiding the topic of her secret work crush. "I guess you could say I'm just curious about your love life."

"All right, let's see if I can give you what you're looking for." Marisa took another drink of her coffee, which no longer burned her tongue. "I don't necessarily have a type. If I'm attracted to someone, then I'm attracted to them. Blondes, brunettes, redheads, or even women with purple hair." She laughed, then shrugged.

"Small, tall, dark, light, short, frumpy. All of the above. Things like that don't matter. Deal breakers—hmmm, that's a toughie. I guess the major dealbreaker is if they don't like kids. I couldn't be with someone that didn't love kids. Besides that, nothing stands out. I don't know that I could be with a smoker, but I might be able to get past it."

Why hadn't she mentioned the age gap issue? She had been adamant about not pursuing younger women, but somehow that was changing.

"So, like, your relationship with Shana…" Samantha's words trailed off.

Marisa looked up, waiting for Samantha to continue.

"You both seemed to mesh well together."

Marisa snickered. "We seemed to mesh well together because we did mesh well together. We had just enough differences to keep the relationship interesting. All around, though, we were similar in a lot of ways. We were the same age, had the same style, same mood, same likes, same dislikes…"

Her mind went to Shana, and she shrugged. "Well, other than the fact that she hated coffee. Couldn't understand that one." Marisa held her mug up and took a drink. "Have to have some differences, though. Things would have gotten awfully boring."

"You mention age a lot," Samantha replied.

Marisa shrugged and looked down at the coffee.

"I always thought age was merely a number, but you seem to focus your attention on that."

"Guess I just realize that if your maturity levels differ, things would never work out."

"But can't someone be emotionally mature, yet physically youthful?"

Marisa sighed. "That's true, but I guess I never considered getting physically attached to someone who wasn't within arm's reach of my age. It just never was something I considered."

"Interesting," Samantha mumbled. "So, then, where do you stand as far as the age gap goes? Five years? Ten years? Won't date anyone past sixty? Younger than thirty? Where does it end?"

"Well, now I think you're just reaching." Marisa laughed. "I mean, I never thought about it in terms of I'll only date those who are thirty-five and older, or they can't be older than fifty. Things like that don't cross my mind. I would say sixty is a little too old, though. Don't want a mother."

Marisa smirked, taking a drink from her coffee mug. "I would say somewhere around five years. So, they have to be thirty-seven to forty-seven. Sounds like a good compromise."

Marisa nodded, feeling good about that decision but knowing that struck out the only woman who had brought her some satisfaction in her fantasies. Though Liz was making her question her stance, she needed to stay true to herself.

"I think if you go along those lines, though, you could in

essence miss out on a great woman," Samantha argued, glancing at Marisa's lips. "If you hit it off with someone, then that should really be the only thing that matters. I just think people get too caught up with caring how old someone is."

"So, we're back to that, huh? This guy must be either super old compared to you or super young. In your case I would say that eighty is way too old and I wouldn't go younger than eighteen. Mainly because you don't want to have to deal with his parents." Marisa snickered, finishing off the rest of her coffee. She got up from the table and went back to the coffee pot. "Do you need another cup?"

"No, I'm fine," Samantha softly replied. "I really don't think you understand where I'm taking this."

Marisa turned to look at Samantha. Samantha's eyes diverted to Marisa's now-empty seat. "I had the perfect birthday planned in my mind."

"What was it?" Marisa asked.

Samantha's phone rang, cutting into the tension in the kitchen, and Samantha groaned and grabbed it from her pocket. She shook her head. "Hello?"

Marisa turned back to her coffee and finished pouring herself a cup.

"Where's Brett?" Samantha asked. "Come on, Chelle. Are you sure?"

Marisa turned back to find Samantha getting up from the table. "I'm on my way. I said I'm on my way. Bye."

"Everything okay?" Marisa asked.

"My sister thinks she's in labor. I have to go."

"Do you need me to follow you or something?" Marisa reached for her car keys, but Samantha shook her head.

"I'm fine. We'll talk later. Thanks for tonight and the Twinkie."

Marisa followed Samantha out of the kitchen and to the front door. "Happy birthday!" Marisa said, hugging Samantha goodbye.

It may have been her imagination, but it seemed like Samantha lingered too long in the embrace. When she pulled back, she hesitated, staring into Marisa's eyes intensely.

Marisa took a step back, and then Samantha gave a quick wave and left. She closed the door once Samantha was out of the driveway. Their conversation replayed in the back of her mind. She got the sense Samantha was trying to tell her something, but what?

Marisa shook her head as she pulled up in front of the club. She wasn't sure why she had even agreed to be there. While several hospital staff wanted to get together for some drinks and fun after work on a Saturday night, she wasn't convinced that she should have agreed to go. This wasn't her scene. The only reason she was going with it was that she knew Hanna would be there and they were the same age. Yet even that seemed like a skewed reason to make her appearance. She hadn't spoken to Hanna since Hanna had awkwardly asked if Marisa was sexually attracted to Liz.

But there were bound to be others in the same age group as her, or at least in the rough vicinity. So, she forced herself to make an appearance. She only needed to have a couple of drinks before deciding to leave.

When she stepped out of the car, she looked down at her attire. She didn't look half bad, at least in her shaky opinion. One thing was certain—she didn't want to cause any friction with the staff, who might be wondering why she wasn't going out with the rest of them.

When she entered the club, she looked around. The music that played over the blaring speakers wasn't a song she recognized but people were already dancing out on the floor, gyrating to the music, like it was the sexual presence that pulled them together.

In two seconds of being there, she considered turning around. Then she spotted Samantha. At least she could have one person to share a pleasant conversation with. On the other side of the floor was Hanna. She was going to avoid her—at least, until she was forced to have another awkward encounter.

She saw others from various floors of the hospital, some she spoke to often, and brief acquaintances whom she didn't have too many conversations with. She waved to a few who looked in her direction.

This wasn't so bad. When a waiter passed, she grabbed a beer from the tray and took a long swig. A few more of those and it might be possible she would forget she didn't want to be there. She took another sip, then cast a glance toward Samantha. She headed over in that direction to talk to her, as she hadn't had the chance in the week since Samantha's birthday. Working opposite shifts had made it difficult to carry on with their interrupted conversation. Plus, she did want to know how things had turned out with Samantha's sister.

"Hey, Marisa. Long time no see."

Marisa stopped when she saw Liz. It wasn't surprising that

Liz was there, but she hesitated briefly. She had done fairly well making sure she didn't have to face Liz, but now there was no avoiding it. Liz was right there. And she looked stunning.

Marisa put on a smile. "Hey. How ya doing?"

"Good," Liz answered. "Over the past week I kind of got the feeling like you've been avoiding me. Funny, right?"

No, because I have been avoiding you. "Not sure I would call it funny, but I guess I wasn't sure if you'd really want to see me. I mean, we didn't really agree on whether you should volunteer and I thought maybe you wouldn't want to see me."

"Oh." Liz stepped back from her, dropping her gaze to the club's floor. "Well, I did start volunteering and I really think it's where I'm needed. If you don't agree with that, then I don't know what to say."

"You don't have to say anything, Liz. If that's how you feel, then great. I'm happy for you if you feel it's the right choice. Really."

Marisa looked over but Samantha had moved somewhere else. She'd have to find her later. "How's Donovan doing?"

"Not great," Liz replied.

Marisa frowned. "He's not? What's going on?"

"I haven't been able to see him. He started chemo this week, and it's taken a toll on his body. Even though I'm volunteering, they only want the actual staff to be around him. So, there's that. Just hoping I can see him soon."

"I'm sorry," Marisa quietly replied. The pain in Liz's eyes was undeniable, and she wanted to pull her into a hug, but that would derail the distance she was putting between them.

"Just praying," Liz replied. "I wanted to talk to you about it but felt that maybe I should give you some space."

"I wouldn't have turned away from your call, Liz. You should know that."

"I do now," Liz said. "Do you want another beer? My treat."

Marisa nodded. "I'd like that."

Maybe Marissa could take a night and just forget about the distance and sexual tension she felt between them. The one-sided sexual tension. She had to constantly remind herself that Liz had a boyfriend and she was straight. Marisa enjoyed Liz's company, so what did it matter if she had one night that she didn't have to think about anything else?

That's what she decided and stuck by as the night went on. She had a few drinks and hung close to Liz. She spotted Hanna looking in their direction a few times, but even that didn't make Marisa pull away. People would believe what they would believe and there wasn't anything that was going to change that. She just wanted to enjoy Liz's company.

"I love this song!" Liz said after they had both emptied their glasses onto a waiter's tray. Before Marisa could fight it, Liz grabbed her hand and pulled her onto the dance floor.

"I don't even know this song!" Marisa yelled over the music.

"Just follow my lead," Liz replied, smiling even wider. Marisa watched her but found it difficult to follow the steps. It didn't seem to matter as they were both laughing and just moving around the floor. The whole dance floor was filled, and everyone seemed to know the dance but Marisa, but that didn't change the fact that she was enjoying herself.

When the song ended, an announcer spoke through the speaker. "Ladies and gents," he started. "As you've been patiently waiting, I'd like to inform you that the entertainment is here and ready to please you all."

Everyone applauded, as did Marisa, but she was still confused. Liz screamed and Marisa frowned. The speakers blared out another song, then in a blur, the dance floor cleared, and five men jumped off a stage and started to dance in front of them. As the crowd cleared to give them room, everyone cheered for the dancers. Liz seemed to be divulging in the cheering louder than most.

Gradually the dancers all scooted around the dance floor, grabbing women who wanted to dance with them. Marisa moved out of the way as one man came up and pulled Liz onto the dance floor. Together they started to dance, with the man grinding against her. Liz was laughing and moving like it was the easiest thing to do.

Marisa looked away, unable to indulge in watching them. Watching Liz act that way and go nuts over male dancers only reminded her of their insurmountable age gap. If this was what Liz wanted, then they would have never gotten a chance to be together. This wasn't something Marisa could see herself getting caught up in and she surely didn't want to watch the woman she was attracted to grinding against a man.

Marisa reached out and grabbed a glass off another tray, tossing some money onto the tray. She took a long sip and tried shaking the image out of her head.

"Not enjoying the show?"

She turned to see Samantha. "Not exactly," Marisa mumbled.

"Yeah, not really my thing either."

Marisa laughed. "Interesting. Another thing I'm learning about you. You're the perfect age for this. I would think you'd be out there with the rest of the young women."

Samantha shrugged.

"I was going to ask you earlier," Marisa continued, "how's your sister? New baby?"

"Nope. It was a false alarm." Samantha laughed, then shrugged again. "A shame I had to leave your house in a rush. Her loser boyfriend, a.k.a. the father of this baby, took off because they got in a fight. I was the only one she could call."

"No need to apologize. It was late anyway. I'm sure you would have had to go sooner than later."

"Would have preferred later," Samantha softly replied. Her words were so low that Marisa thought she heard her wrong. She opened her mouth to ask, but Samantha said, "So, going back to the age gap issue we discussed before. Correct me if I'm wrong, but I would say Liz isn't in the vicinity of what you're looking for."

Marisa snickered. "Your point?" She took a sip of her beer and looked at Samantha.

"Come on, Marisa. It's pretty obvious you're into her. Maybe you don't want to admit that and that's fine, but you can't fool me. Or half of the hospital, for that matter. But then when you see that…"

She pointed to the dance floor, where Liz was now getting a lap dance from the male dancer. "I don't see how you couldn't be turned off and see that she's not the woman for you. Liz is looking pretty into the guy's moves, if you know what I mean. So, why put yourself through the heartache?"

Marisa's stomach churned, but she didn't want to admit that Samantha was right. "And I'll tell you, as I've said before. You're reading the signs wrong."

Samantha nodded. "If only that were true. Then maybe others would have a shot."

Marisa laughed. "Others? I don't see anyone kicking down my door. I'm staying single and I'm fine with that, but I'm telling you that Liz and I are merely friends." *And at this point, I'm not even sure if we're that.*

"Are you just oblivious?" Samantha asked. "You've been around and can surely see the signs that I've been directing your way. And maybe I'm not in your age bracket either. Heck, I'm even younger than she is. But I'm mature for my age. If memory serves me, you've even told me that once or twice. So, sometimes you just need to let nature take its course."

She grabbed onto Marisa's arm and pulled her close. In a matter of seconds, Samantha kissed her, and Marisa wasn't sure if it was the adrenaline rush or the pure shock racing through her system, but she didn't pull back. Even as she could feel everyone's eyes on them, she allowed the kiss to linger. Her mind was mush and suddenly everything she thought she knew was thrown out the window.

CHAPTER TWELVE

Liz

The fresh air hit Liz straight in the face as she wheeled Donovan into the garden. Her hands gripped the handles of the wheelchair, with a picnic basket tucked in the bottom of the chair.

"How's this spot?" she asked, pulling him up. They were right next to the roses, and she could smell the scent coming off the flowers around them. Sadly, they didn't lift her mood. Ever since that night at the club, she had to force smiles and chug energy drinks to get through the day. It felt like storm clouds had rolled in and were drenching her with rain.

"Nice," Donovan said.

When she sat down on the bench next to him, she looked over in his direction. Color had returned to his cheeks. Maybe this was exactly what he needed as part of his treatment. It had been tough getting him out there, but since he had been getting stronger, she had taken the first opportunity to do so.

"Do you want turkey, bologna, or ham?" she asked, digging into the basket.

He laughed. "You brought all that?"

"Are you kidding me? For you, I'd bring the world."

The smile on his face was bright and infectious—certainly, something that couldn't go unnoticed. Liz was so happy that everything worked out. Not only was the weather gorgeous, with a ray of sunlight cascading over the garden, but she had gotten the clear to get him out there. She wouldn't have been able to pull it off if even one person had objected. Victoria was ecstatic for Liz to take him on a picnic, and the doctors all agreed, since he had gone forty-eight hours without barfing. He needed to have fresh air and sunlight in his diet. It'd been almost two weeks since he'd been stuck inside, and that was ten days too long. Everyone—but most of all, Liz—was ready to see him outside of his room. Whatever was going on in her personal life didn't matter. She needed to be here for Donovan.

"Turkey," he said. "No, ham." A sly grin popped on his face. "Bologna?"

Liz laughed. "I know exactly what you need. Give me a minute." She tore three sandwiches apart and put meat from each one until she had made a sandwich piled so high that she wasn't sure he would be able to handle it. She was mistaken as his eyes went wide and he took a bite. He took a moment to chew it, but the grin that played on his face was magnetic.

"This is so good," he said, chomping down on the rest of that bite.

Liz was proud of herself for coming up with something that made Donovan happy. "Glad you like it."

She took a bite of her turkey club, then reached into the basket and pulled out a variety of chips. Donovan was quick to grab a bag of barbecue, and she ripped it open for him.

"Orange or apple juice?" she asked.

"Apple," he said between bites.

They both settled into a routine of just enjoying the meal. They were the only two out there, so it was a great, relaxing experience, and Liz, for one, couldn't take it for granted. Donovan wasn't the only one who needed that. She took a bite of her sandwich, then popped a chip into her mouth.

When she looked over at Donovan, his eyes were drawn to his food, and he looked uneasy. His lips were curved into a frown. Liz hesitated but couldn't hold off any longer. "Everything okay, bud?" she asked. "You're not sick now, are you? Too much food?"

He shook his head, then looked up. "No. I'm good. But thank you. This means a lot to me."

He turned his gaze away from her, and she followed his eyes as he scanned the garden. "You're the only one…"

He stopped talking, then took in a deep breath. Liz reached out and touched his shoulder, waiting for him to continue. "The only one who doesn't treat me like I'm going to break. It's nice."

Liz reached out and touched his knee. "Remember when we spoke that first night at the hospital? I said a mother's job is to worry, or something like that. But if you feel like your mom is all over you, you should talk to her. She only means the best."

"I don't want to make her sad. She cries enough."

He took a bite of his sandwich. Liz understood that. It was

tough having to watch the one you love suffer. And if something happened to take away that life, it left you a shell of yourself. She had seen that firsthand with her own mother.

"Donovan, your mother would hate to know you're feeling this way. You should talk to her. Trust me."

He nodded, then grinned. "Look at this."

He put the small bag of chips up to his mouth and downed them in one swoop. He laughed as he munched on the crumbs that were left. That was what Liz liked to see. She wanted to see him in his element, being a kid, laughing and enjoying himself. So far, she was succeeding.

"I can do that, too," Liz said, flipping the bag up and pouring the crumbs into her mouth.

Donovan's eyes went wide, and his face went red as he continued to laugh. He then started to choke, and Liz's laughter died.

"Are you okay?" she jumped up and considered pulling him out of the chair and doing the Heimlich if needed, but he started to laugh again, easing her mind.

"Got you," he said.

"Donovan Prescott! That wasn't even funny."

He giggled, wadding his napkin up and tossing it at her. Looking at him at that moment, no one would have been able to guess that he was sick. It had been several days since Liz had last been able to see him, and from what the doctors and Mindi had said, he was so sick that they weren't sure he'd ever regain his strength while fighting through the chemo treatments. Through the prayers, it looked like something was actually working.

Liz turned to look toward the garden entrance just as another person stepped out toward the roses. *Marisa*. As their eyes locked, Liz inhaled sharply, her insides a mix of butterflies. There was a squeezing pressure on her chest. She broke eye contact, looking down.

She hadn't seen Marisa since the Saturday night at the club. She still couldn't shake the image that played through her mind as Marisa and Samantha made out in front of everyone. It was awkward, but everyone else seemed to be happy to cheer it on.

Liz had felt ready to cry.

Seeing that kiss had changed something in her. She had no idea Samantha and Marisa were involved with each other, and it filled her with envy. In that moment, she had realized she wanted to be the one Marisa kissed. She wanted to know how Marisa's lips felt and what it would be like to trace her hands along the curves of her hips.

She had slipped out of the club silently and went home to lie in bed, awake all night, staring at the ceiling. She'd never felt this way for another woman. What did that mean for her and Chad? What about the age difference? The gap didn't matter to Liz, but was it a problem for Marisa?

As Liz's cheeks burned, Marisa cleared her throat.

"Oh. I'm sorry. I didn't know anyone was out here." She started to turn away.

Liz felt a strong urge to just let Marisa go back inside, but she didn't own the garden and it wasn't her place to turn her away. "No need to rush off. We were just enjoying the scenery."

Liz glanced at Donovan, whose joyful and mischievous demeanor had suddenly become reserved. She remembered all too well how he had appeared shy and recluse when they had first met. "Marisa? This is Donovan. Donovan, Marisa."

Marisa smiled, then nodded. "We met. When I did his blood, remember?"

Liz's cheeks flamed up. How could she have been so dumb? Of course they knew one another. And here she thought she was being considerate by introducing the two.

She covered her face. "Oy, duh."

Marisa smiled. "How ya doing, Donovan?"

"Good," Donovan said. "Liz made lunch!"

His eyes brightened, and he didn't look reserved any longer. Maybe he was afraid that Marisa would stick him with more needles.

"Cold meat sandwiches." Liz shrugged. "Nothing major."

Marisa gave her a genuine smile, then looked over to Donovan. "That's nice. You're looking good. I heard you haven't been feeling too well, so I'm glad to see you looking well."

She knelt next to him, and Liz caught herself watching their sweet encounter. While Marisa talked to Donovan, Liz moved her eyes to look at Marisa. There was a light behind Marisa's blue eyes, and it choked Liz.

She quickly diverted her eyes down to her hands. Why she got caught up staring at this woman's eyes was beyond her. But they had slowly gotten closer over the weeks. Yet, some moments seem to separate them, such as the club. They had been getting along, so she thought. Then Marisa had gone off to Samantha and started kissing her in front of everyone. It left Liz confused. Marisa didn't seem the type.

"Are you guys best friends?" Donovan asked, tearing Liz's eyes back to him.

Marisa turned and met Liz's gaze, her lips in a straight line.

On one hand, she looked to be smiling with her eyes, yet her gaze was also blank.

It was Marisa who spoke up. "Liz is a very good person. Anyone would be glad to have a best friend like that." That was an easy response. "Do you have a best friend?" she continued.

Liz released a breath. Getting his attention off them was the best route to turn.

"Joey," Donovan replied simply. "Haven't seen him since I got here. I miss him."

"And I'm sure he misses you, too," Marisa softly replied. She stood to her feet. "I have to get back to work. But it was good to see you." She rested her hand on his shoulder before turning to Liz. "Both of you."

"Good to see you," Liz replied, standing up from the bench. "We have to get back inside as well."

"Do we have to?" Donovan groaned.

"Sorry, buddy." Liz smiled. "We'll do this again sometime."

"Do you wanna come, Marisa?" Donovan asked, piping in.

Liz opened her mouth to break off that suggestion right away, but before she could, Marisa smiled and nodded her head. Liz snapped her mouth shut, then kept her eyes off Marisa as she said, "I'll be sure to let you know when we do this again."

It was probably best not to have Marisa tag along next time. What if Liz's feelings started to become more obvious before she even had a chance to make sense of them?

"Sounds good. You both take care." Marisa walked past her, and Liz turned to watch her leave. She was gone before Liz could utter a response.

"I like her," Donovan said.

"Yeah, she's nice." Liz turned back to look at him and grab

the items to put back in the picnic basket. "Are you ready to head back in?"

"No," he grumbled.

Liz smirked and piled the basket into the bottom of his wheelchair. She couldn't wait until they got back out there or even went down to the cafeteria again. Just getting Donovan out of his room was something that Liz would continue to do whenever she got the chance.

When they got back up to his room, Victoria was still sitting next to his bed. Her eyes were closed, and Liz maneuvered him so that she wouldn't wake up. However, as he slipped into the bed, Victoria moved. She opened her eyes, and Liz cringed.

"Sorry. We tried to be quiet."

Victoria shook her head and sat up straighter. "No problem. Did you guys have a good time?"

"It was beautiful, Momma," Donovan eagerly replied. "You should see it sometime."

"I'll do my best." She shot a look at Liz and mouthed, *Thank you!*

Liz nodded and moved closer to the bed. "I'd better get out of here. I have some things to do once I get home."

"How are things with volunteering and your full-time job?" Victoria asked. "I'm sure you have little time to do anything else."

"Enjoying every minute of it. Wouldn't trade it for anything."

Liz meant it, but she was also exhausted. Sometimes, she was so exhausted that she caught herself falling asleep in the parking lot before she could even get home. Yet, she really didn't want to change anything about that.

"Just glad to do what I'm doing," she replied. "I'll see you both around."

She waved and then left Donovan's room. Before she headed to the elevator, she stopped at Gina's room. Gina was the newest patient brought into the ward, newly diagnosed with Wilms' tumor, a kidney cancer. She knocked and waited for someone to call out to let her enter.

"Yes?" Gina's mother's voice echoed through the door.

Liz peeked her head inside. "Just heading out but wanted to see if either of you wanted or needed anything."

Gina, who had just celebrated her tenth birthday the previous day, put on a weak smile. "I'm fine," she mumbled. Her eyes were tearing up, and that wasn't because of a side effect of cancer. Liz knew she had interrupted at the worst possible time.

She walked into the room and brushed her hand against the girl's forehead. "Heard they got a new flavor of pudding," Liz offered.

Gina shook her head. "Stomach feels sick."

"All right, honey. If you need anything, your mother has my number. Have a good evening."

She looked over at Gina's mother. It wasn't easy seeing so much pain in children, but Liz knew this was the absolute thing she needed to focus her attention on. Knowing that she could help kids in a volunteer capacity when she wasn't working made her feel fulfilled, as if she had been given a unique opportunity.

Liz left the hospital, and a weight lifted off her shoulders. Donovan was getting the care he needed, and that was what she had to believe in—the power of a doctor's hands. She got into her car and sighed, leaning back against the car seat.

Her phone rang, and she pulled it out of her pocket. Chad's

name flashed on the screen. She had been working hard to ignore all his calls, knowing it was only pulling them further apart. But how could she face him considering she'd developed an attraction for someone else?

"Hello?"

"Is this Liz? Really?" Chad laughed. "Didn't think I would ever reach my love."

Liz remained silent.

"I imagine you must be working hard on wedding preparations."

That hadn't really entered her mind, but telling him so would surely put another wedge between them. "Work has been rough," Liz replied. "And I'm doing some volunteering in the cancer ward for children. But I sent that to you in text."

"Right. I recall seeing that."

You do? Because I don't recall getting a text back commenting on the matter.

"Yeah, so it's kept me occupied."

Liz looked down at her unadorned finger. The thought of promising her love to him for the rest of her life wasn't even on the forefront of her mind, and it killed her. If she said yes to a marriage proposal, she wanted to believe that it would always be forever. Yet she just wanted to figure a way out.

A tear dropped from the corner of her eye, and she quickly flicked it away. "How's France?"

"Good. Busy. We're close to a deal, though. It shouldn't be too much longer. Doing what I can to get home to my baby."

She forced a smile, but when it wouldn't touch the corner of her lips, she felt a pit growing in her stomach. "I'm sorry, Chad.

I have to get back to work. Only had a few minutes to take this call."

"Oh. Sure. Well, I hope we can truly talk in the next few days. Maybe we can video chat."

"Yep, sounds good. Talk later." Liz quickly disconnected the call.

She wanted to grow stronger in love with her fiancé, but with him gone, it only cemented their distance, which was hard to overcome. It also didn't help when every facet of her life was now surrounded by anything but planning for a life of marriage. Donovan needed her attention, for one.

Liz's mind shifted back to Marisa, the one adult she could tell her troubles to and not fear that she would be questioned or judged. But Marisa had her own life and her own romantic relationships and Liz wanted to respect that. All she needed was to find a way back to the easiness she felt when Marisa and she were just growing as friends. And to get rid of all these strange feelings that seeing that kiss had stirred in her.

Without her friendship with Marisa, she felt like she lost everything. That fact scared her even more.

Liz was sitting on her couch, staring at Marisa's name on her phone. Should she call or not? That was the question that had been in her mind for two days now. After seeing Marisa in the garden, she knew that she wanted to hold on to their friendship above all else. She needed to chat with someone about her relationship with Chad, because at that moment she was confused and conflicted about how she wanted to work out her engagement woes.

She sighed and finally made the call. A text would have been better, but it was way too informal to resolve the situation. The phone rang several times and then went to Marisa's voicemail.

"You've reached Marisa. I'm away from my phone, so leave me a message. I'll return your call as soon as I'm able."

The beep sounded. "Hey, Marisa, it's Liz. So, just thought I'd reach out and see what you're doing tonight. Thought we could get together and chat about something. No rush to call me back. Just—if you're available. Talk soon."

She hung up and stared at her phone. It was all in Marisa's hand from that point on. If she didn't call back, then she knew that Marisa wasn't interested in working on their friendship.

Thirty minutes later, Liz's phone rang; Marisa's name flashed on the screen.

"Hey, Liz," Marisa replied after Liz answered the phone. "Sorry I missed your call. As for tonight, I'd like that, but I work until eight. It'd be a late dinner but if you're up for it, we could meet at the cafeteria."

The cafeteria didn't appeal to Liz, as she knew that they could be interrupted and overheard by other employees.

"Eight o'clock would be fine, but what about meeting at Char's right down the block? If that doesn't work we could do the cafeteria, but just thought this would be different."

"I'm fine with that," Marisa commented. "I'll see you no later than eight-thirty."

"I'll be there waiting. See you then!"

Liz hung up the call, got up from the couch, and headed to her room. Now to just think about what to wear. She didn't want to wear anything that would be revealing, but she also didn't want to look frumpy. After cycling through several outfits, she opted for blue jeans and a simple pink blouse. Then she spent way too much time than was necessary on her makeup and hair.

Looking at herself in the mirror, she frowned. *What am I doing? We're just hanging out as friends. Just friends.*

She misted her hair so the curls loosened and then tied her hair in a ponytail. Then she wiped off some of the makeup. She wasn't going on a date. Just meeting a *friend*. She was dressed an hour early, but at least she was prepared ahead of time.

The clock ticked slowly by, but that was to be expected. She had a list in her mind of everything she wanted to get off her chest. For starters, it was time to tell someone about her engagement. To make it real. Sure, she and Chad had some things to work out, but she cared for him. They had been together a while, so it was probably time to move the relationship forward. Getting the engagement out in the open might help bring back some of their spark, and she might start to feel close to him again. What she felt for Marisa were just feelings. She didn't need to act on them. She needed to turn her focus back to Chad and her relationship with him.

Despite her thoughts, her heart wasn't convinced that was what she really wanted.

She dropped the engagement ring in a pocket of her purse and left for dinner.

At eight-fifteen Liz walked into the restaurant. Marisa was already seated in the corner booth, her eyes locked down on the menu. She went to the table and Marisa looked up.

"Hey."

"You're here early," Liz replied, taking her seat.

"Wanted to make sure I got out of there. Sometimes the lab gets backed up and I end up staying longer. When Angie got in, I told her I had to finish up paperwork and needed to get out of there. Your call sounded important." She closed her menu and slid it over to Liz.

Liz grabbed it and opened it, but then closed it right back up. "Didn't mean for it to sound that eager."

She snickered, though, in truth, she had been pretty eager. Getting out the truth was going to be a weight lifted off her and she was anticipating that moment. If Marisa were a true friend, then she would understand where Liz came from and why Liz had kept Chad's engagement from everyone.

A waitress walked up to the table. "Are you ready to order?" she asked. "The name is Tiff, and I can start you out with drinks."

"I'll just take water," Liz said.

"Same." Marisa nodded in agreement.

Tiff left and Liz turned back to Marisa. "How was work?"

Marisa heaved a sigh. "Some days I think it's time to retire, but it was all right."

Liz dropped her purse on the spot next to her in the booth. "I have a ways to go before I can even dream of retirement. But, hey, I have some days like that, too."

Marisa nodded, but her eyes shifted to where Tiff stood with their waters. They placed their orders, and once Tiff left again, Liz knew it was time she should just get it out there. She felt it would be better to say everything at the beginning of the meal, giving Marisa time to process it and discuss why Liz was so hesitant about Chad.

"So," she started.

"I was surprised to get your call," Marisa said, interrupting her. Liz looked away from her purse and back to Marisa. "After the club, I thought maybe something had changed with you. It just seemed like you didn't want to talk to me. I saw you a few times in the cafeteria and once in the breakroom and you totally ignored me."

"I did?" Liz asked. "I'll be honest, I don't recall seeing you. If anything, I thought maybe we were just on opposite schedules. While we used to bump into one another often, it didn't seem to be the case anymore. Then I thought maybe you were avoiding me because..."

"Because why?" Marisa asked.

Liz shrugged. "I don't know, really. Maybe because everyone from the hospital saw you." She latched down on her lip. "You know, at the club."

"Oh. You mean with Samantha?" Liz nodded and Marisa's cheeks turned a shade of red. "That wasn't supposed to happen."

"It doesn't matter. You don't have to explain it to me. You can kiss whoever you want to kiss."

"But, Liz, hear me out," Marisa started. "I didn't want to. I mean, it wasn't me..." Her words trailed off as Liz took a drink of her water.

Somehow the conversation had flipped to the kiss and Liz wanted to shift it quickly. She wasn't there to ridicule Marisa for kissing someone. If they were having a secret rendezvous, she couldn't judge her. She didn't want to judge her.

"Please. That's not why I came here," Liz pleaded. "The truth is, I had something to tell you and wanted to get it out there before we got too far into dinner. That's all, and it wasn't because I felt the need to talk about Samantha. Wasn't even in my thoughts."

That was a lie. Truthfully, Liz couldn't get the kiss out of her mind. She couldn't stop thinking about switching places with Samantha and…

She shook her head. That's not why she wanted to talk to Marisa. She needed to focus.

"There's just something I wanted to talk to you about so I can get your advice. That's all."

Marisa nodded as their food arrived. "Thank you," Marisa said to Tiff.

"Thank you," Liz added softly.

When Tiff was gone, Marisa looked down at her food.

"Ever try the fish here?"

"Nope. I'm a pretty plain person." Liz pointed to her plate. "I'll take chicken any day, but the fish looks good."

Marisa smiled, which tugged at Liz's heart. Suddenly all conversation about Samantha ended, along with thoughts of speaking about Chad. She bit her bottom lip, trying not to stare at Marisa and how pretty she looked.

"So, while I really didn't mean to ignore you at the hospital, it really was an oversight. I was so focused on Donovan's health that my mind didn't seem to be all there over the past week. If I blatantly ignored you, or you thought I saw you and I just didn't greet you, I apologize. If we cross paths, I wouldn't intentionally ignore you. That's not my style."

Marisa nodded. "Well, if I was worried about it, I should have come over to you. So, for that, I'm just as to blame." Marisa took a bite of her fish and Liz watched her.

"Good?"

"Excellent." Marisa took another bite, then continued. "But on a better note, Donovan looked good when I saw you both a couple days ago."

"He looks stronger than I expected. I was happy about that. And I was super happy I was able to take him outside. He needed it. I needed it."

"Do you know what his treatment plan is going to be?" Marisa asked.

"I know that they're doing chemo every other week. That will hopefully get him to feeling much stronger when he has to have his next one."

"That's good and promising. Still keeping him in my prayers."

"Thank you!" Liz took a bite of her potato, then another bite of her chicken. Talking to Marisa was easy. She didn't have to think about what she was saying, she just could be herself. *Maybe now isn't the right time to mention Chad. I will in a little bit…*

She just wanted to have this moment in which they could talk back and forth like they used to before things got complicated.

They shifted the conversation to the weather and even that didn't seem strange. It was relaxing and Liz cherished it. When the meal was close to coming to an end, with neither one having much on their plates, Liz took a sip of her water and swallowed the lump that had come back to her throat. It was time. She reached into her purse to pull out her ring.

"So, can I be honest with you about something that's been nagging at me?" Marisa asked, dropping her napkin in front of Liz.

Liz dropped the ring from her finger, and it went back into the pocket. "Sure. What is it?"

A reprieve from having to divulge her own deepest secrets.

"So, I've worked with Samantha for over three years and never saw her as anything more than a coworker, with the potential for being a friend. We just weren't that way. For one, she just turned twenty-two. That's way too young. With that twenty-year age gap, the thought of being with her in any way other than a friend has never crossed my mind."

"Marisa, you don't have to explain."

"But I do. Stepping into that club on Saturday night, I was reminded just how much older than everyone I am."

Liz smiled. "Stop it. You're not old." She quickly realized that Marisa wasn't laughing. Her seriousness wiped the smile from Liz's face.

"I'm older than all of you. And when those dancers—strippers, really—came out on the floor and all of you were gyrating against them…"

Liz tilted her head. "We were having fun. Nothing happened. Our clothes were still on."

Marisa nodded. "I'm not a prude, or never thought I was. But in that moment, I felt uncomfortable on so many levels." She shrugged. "It just hit me that I didn't belong."

"Don't feel that way," Liz quickly interjected, trying to get through to Marisa. "You belonged just as much as anyone else did. I know many people were happy you were there."

Marisa shook her head, and Liz paused. She thought she would get through her soon enough, but Marisa continued.

"So, when I was talking to Samantha, she said that however I felt about age at that moment wasn't a big deal because she had feelings for me. Then she kissed me. That's how it went down. I didn't expect it and I definitely didn't want it. I was taken aback, so, yeah, I let it linger. But the thing is, in the perfect world, I would have wanted to be there kissing someone else. If age weren't a factor, it wouldn't have been Samantha that I would've chosen. Sometimes you just do things because it's easier than stopping them."

Liz frowned. So, Marisa wanted someone else, but age was a factor? "Have you talked to this woman?"

Marisa snickered. "That's why I like you, Liz. There's a certain naïveté about you. In many ways I'm just as naïve."

Liz furrowed her brows. *What is she getting at?*

"It's you, Liz. And I know you have a boyfriend, and the age would never be something we could get over, but I'm forced to be honest. I just hope one day you can understand that you can't help who you find attractive. Furthermore, I hope you realize that I can put my feelings aside and I hope that we can somehow find our way back to a friendship."

Liz's jaw dropped as she processed what she'd just heard. How could she have missed this? Chad was struck from her mind; she no longer had any intention of bringing up that conversation to Marisa. She was struggling to find the words to speak.

"I'm sorry," Marisa whispered. "You don't have to say anything."

Liz watched as Marisa tossed some money down on the table and stood up from the booth. "Sorry," she said again.

She then hurried out of the restaurant.

Liz stared at the empty space in front of her, Marisa's bombshell playing on a continuous loop in her head. She closed her mouth and looked over her shoulder, but Marisa was gone. *Marisa!* They had to talk about this. She tossed some money down on the table as well, way more than what would pay for the bill, then grabbed her purse and ran out of the restaurant.

Outside, it had started raining, and Liz glanced around the full parking lot but couldn't see Marisa anywhere. How could she go home and just ignore what Marisa had laid out on her? She walked back to her car, her head foggy with disbelief.

She unlocked the door and started to open it when she heard her name. "Liz!"

Liz turned and Marisa stood inches from her. Without another word, she pulled Liz toward her and kissed her. Liz dropped her purse and, without hesitation, wrapped her arms around Marisa and just let Marisa's tongue slip into her mouth and take over all her cognitive senses.

Liz gasped and Marisa pulled back from the kiss. "I couldn't leave without doing that."

She turned and walked away from Liz. Only two words came to Liz's mind. *Come back!*

But Marisa was already gone.

CHAPTER THIRTEEN

Marisa

If Marisa had gotten a phone call from Liz, then she would have at least felt better leaving her with the kiss still haunting her lips. She had gone back for a kiss to see if she would feel anything coming from Liz. She had. Liz had responded, giving reason enough to tell Marisa that maybe the age difference wouldn't interfere with a potential relationship. But not once had Liz called her or even texted her. A response would have been nice, but Marisa knew what was going through Liz's mind.

There was a light tap on her office door and Marisa looked up to see Samantha. A week had gone by and she had been able to avoid Samantha after the kiss at the club. Ironically, while she had anticipated a call from Liz, one would imagine that Samantha was doing the same with Marisa. She stayed silent because she didn't want to face the awkwardness that would ensue from the aftermath of the kiss.

She knew the truth already. She didn't have to debate over it. Samantha was a nice woman, but that wasn't where her heart leaned. If she were going to be with someone, regardless of age, she would embrace her feelings for Liz. Samantha was a year younger than that, and it was foolish to go with something just because someone else wanted you to. She couldn't hide her feelings for someone else, despite what Samantha wanted. Besides, in the three years she knew her, never once had Samantha expressed being into women. So, maybe she just wanted to experiment, but Marisa wasn't the type to be with someone who wasn't ready to go all in.

"Hey," Marisa said, slipping her hands into her pockets. "Thought Brooke was working the front desk today."

"She was but went home sick. So you're stuck with me."

Marisa nodded. "Is my next patient out there?" She moved toward the door.

Samantha reached out and touched her arm, making Marisa slip her gaze to Samantha's.

"Are we going to talk about it?" Samantha inquired.

If Marisa had her way, then she would rather not hash over what had happened. She couldn't change it, and it was best just to ignore it altogether.

"I don't know what to say," Marisa admitted. "Do you really feel something?"

"Yeah," Samantha said. "I've been trying to deny it, but those feelings are there and to deny them would be denying who I am. I don't want to do that any longer. I'm sorry if that puts you in a strange situation, but I'm just trying to be honest."

"Look, Samantha," Marisa started. "I appreciate that you're trying to put your feelings out there and you're a great woman, but…"

"You have feelings for someone else," Samantha proceeded.

"Believe me, I'm trying to fight that. With our age difference, it's not going to pan out well. So, I'm doing everything I can to ignore those feelings. But with you, I would still have the age difference."

And then the kiss happened with Liz and now I'm not sure what's going to happen.

When Samantha had kissed Marisa, there were sparks of passion there, but Marisa's heart wasn't fully into it. The kiss with Liz, however, had electrified her. It was like fireworks and hard to ignore.

"I don't want to hurt you, but if I'm being honest…" Her words trailed off. However she spelled it out to Samantha, she was destined to say the wrong thing.

"It's just that if I choose to pursue something with you, it would be because I didn't want to be alone, and you deserve way better than that."

Samantha nodded. "Maybe I should have talked to you when I first started getting these feelings, and then maybe I wouldn't have put myself through all this." She shrugged. "I'll get over it."

The bell rang at the front desk and Samantha moved toward the door of her office. "I had better get to my patient."

"I'll prep them. Thank you."

Samantha left the office and Marisa sunk back down in her desk chair. It wasn't the hardest conversation she had ever had.

That would come if she could ever talk to Liz. She got up from her chair and went to prepare the lab for her patient.

The day turned busy after that patient, and it left her little time to think about Liz and the kiss and what the kiss meant. That was the good thing as far as that went. She cleaned the lab down from the previous patient when she spotted Samantha peeking her head into the lab.

"You have a call on line two," she said. "Children's oncology ward."

"All right. Thanks!" She grabbed the phone and hit the line. "This is Marisa."

"Hello, this is Jamie, a volunteer on floor four, children's oncology. I'm calling because we have a patient who needs lab work done."

"Patient name?" Marisa asked.

"Donovan Prescott."

Marisa looked up from her computer. *Donovan?*

"Have the orders been entered into the computer?"

"As far as I know. I'm just a volunteer."

"All right. I'll be right there."

Marisa looked up the orders on the computer. She decided she wouldn't bother to alert the phlebotomist and would draw the blood herself. She grabbed her supplies, then hurried past the front desk. "I have an urgent draw. I'll be right back."

Her breath hitched as she got on the elevator. She was anxious to get upstairs, as she was just as worried about Donovan as Liz was. The elevator seemed to sneak up the floors, but finally, the door opened. When she got off, she spotted Mindi at the desk.

"That was quick," Mindi said.

"Had a lull in patients." Marisa shrugged. "Donovan needs his blood drawn? Do you know why? This seems sudden. I hope he's okay."

"Yeah, they're looking at transferring him to the university hospital. They're going to enroll him in a clinical trial. The specialists at the hospital want an updated set of labs. He's in there." She motioned to the room.

Marisa considered what she had just heard, then looked back to Mindi. "Does Liz know he might be transferring?"

She shrugged. "Not sure. Excuse me, it's been a hectic day."

She then rushed off as Marisa turned back to Donovan's room. She knocked on the door, then entered the room. Donovan looked over at her, a wide smile on his face.

"Marisa!"

"Hey, bud," Marisa said, walking over and hugging him. She looked over to Victoria, who was beaming. That was a good sign. She knew that Victoria was emotional whenever given uncertain news, so it was a blessing that she didn't appear upset. "You know the drill. This will only take a second."

She pulled the cart over to the bed and Victoria reached out for her son's hand. Marisa would get the blood drawn and call Liz to make certain Liz knew that Donovan might be relocated. She knew that Liz would want to be there to say her goodbyes. She decided to finish off her schedule and then worry about talking to Liz later.

When her shift ended, Marisa walked out of the hospital and sighed as the cool air hit her face. She loved the spring air, when it was much warmer than winter and not as hot and humid as the summer months. She pulled her jacket tight across her chest and headed off toward her car. As she stepped into the parking lot, she spotted Liz walking no more than ten feet in front of her.

She thought about what she needed to tell her about Donovan and decided it was just as good a time as any. "Liz!" she called out.

Liz hesitated and turned to look over her shoulder. Marisa picked up her pace to meet up with her, but Liz turned and moved faster to get away. When it was evident that Marisa wouldn't reach her before she got in her car and drove away, she stopped trying. Liz got into her vehicle and hurried off, leaving Marisa literally in her dust.

Marisa didn't want to be upset by Liz's reaction. She understood that kissing her was out of a brief lapse in judgment. Yet, down in her gut, she had this gnawing feeling and felt like she had ruined everything. She wanted a chance at friendship, but there was looking to be little chance of that.

CHAPTER FOURTEEN

Liz

Liz woke and rolled over in her bed, staring out the window. She could still hear Marisa calling out for her and running up behind her, like Liz couldn't wait to have a chat with her. How could Marisa expect Liz to be open for discussion when Liz could barely process the thoughts that the kiss had brought up?

You wanted the kiss, Liz. Just admit that.

Her subconscious was smarter than she was. Yes, she had wanted the kiss. What was even harder to admit was that she had needed the kiss. She had needed to feel Marisa's desire for her. It freaked her out in many ways. Marisa was the only one who made her feel seen and accepted as she was, and she now longed to explore her feelings for Marisa in a physical way.

Liz got up from the bed and went over to her jewelry box.

After digging through her box, she realized her ring wasn't there.

"Where could it have…" Her words trailed off as she left her room. She had forgotten she had stuffed it away in her purse when she had intended on clarifying things with Marisa and telling her the secret she had been hiding.

Downstairs, her purse still lay on the couch, where she had left it when she first got home. She grabbed it and plopped down on the couch, then dug through the purse into the compartment she had placed the ring. She pulled her finger out, but the ring wasn't there. Liz tipped her purse over and slid her hands around, looking for the one thing she needed to have back in her possession desperately.

Gone. In just ten minutes of frantically digging, she was positive that the ring was no longer in the purse. For good measure, she went back through the contents again, then dug through the crevices of the purse. Nothing.

Liz cupped her mouth, stunned that she had lost the exorbitantly priced ring. Chad was one to brag about spending his money, and while she didn't know the exact amount, she was confident enough to believe that he had spared no expenses when deciding to propose to his wife.

Liz felt the tears coming. She covered her eyes and closed them tightly, willing herself not to let any tears fall down her cheeks.

He would understand, right? No. How would he possibly understand that I wasn't wearing my ring? He's going to know something is wrong. He's going to think I'm having second thoughts about this whole thing.

Her hand fell from her face, and she stared straight ahead, even more confused than before. She was having all sorts of doubts, and it wasn't a huge leap to think that he would think those things.

The last place she knew she had it was at the restaurant. It was a long shot that anyone would actually turn the ring in, but maybe some saint had come across the ring and decided to do the right thing.

Liz called the restaurant, waited for someone to answer. Finally, a woman came on the line. Liz released a breath as the woman greeted her.

"Hi, so I have a crazy request. I lost a ring when I was there the other day. I just realized it's missing, and it's the last place I know for certain I had it. Someone didn't by chance turn it in, did they?"

"A ring did get turned in. Just a minute; I'll go double check on that."

Liz's breath hitched. Was it possible? This would be the best news ever if they truly had her ring. She waited for the woman to return to the line. It felt like forever, but finally, she came back on the line.

"Sorry for the delay."

"No worries. Do you have it?" Liz held her breath.

"Yep. We have a ring. It's a mood ring, right?" the woman asked.

The minute she said that, Liz's heart fell. She was seconds from thinking that something was actually working in her favor, but now there was little hope.

"Actually, no. But that's all you got?"

Liz hated that her hopes were dashed, but it wasn't the woman's fault. She was destined to have to tell Chad that some-thing tragic had happened.

"Yeah. Sorry," she said. "I can take your name if something turns up."

Liz rattled off her number, then quickly hung up. It was hopeless and there was only one thing she could do. It was either bite the bullet and do it now or wait until they were face to face. That was an easy decision to make. She didn't want to see Chad in front of her as she told him she had lost her engagement ring. She pulled up his name and dialed his number.

The phone rang three times and was just about to reach voicemail when someone answered.

"Hello?"

Liz's mouth hung open as a woman's voice echoed through the phone. It came again. "Hello? Anyone there?"

"Babe, who's on the phone?" Chad asked. The sound of running water sounded in the background and Liz held her breath, waiting for some sort of plausible explanation.

"Guess nobody," she said, then the phone went dead.

Nobody? She had to have seen the name flashing on the screen of his phone. Did she not know who Liz was? More than that, who was *she*? One thing was for certain. When Chad came back, they had a lot to talk about—none of which about how excited she was for their nuptials. At this rate, the likelihood of marrying Chad just kept getting lower and lower.

TEARS STUNG LIZ'S EYES AS SHE SAT HUDDLED UP IN THE CORNER of her couch, distraught over hearing the woman's voice. She groaned and sat up, rubbing her eyes raw, trying to get rid of her tears. Who cared if Chad was sleeping around on her? It wasn't like she hadn't considered just calling the whole thing off. She hesitated, that thought still looping through her mind. It was true. The thought had crossed her mind every day since she had accepted his proposal. *If you're not happy, then run.*

Still, the mere thought that Chad was out there having sex with another woman had Liz's skin crawling. Mostly because of the deception behind it. He must've wanted to marry her. Otherwise, why go through the charade? His mom expected it? She supposed that was plausible.

She got up from the couch and started frantically pacing back and forth. She was upset that she had practically caught them in bed together. The fact that she had heard the woman had her skin crawling, and she shivered, pulling her arms across her stomach, which felt queasy, and holding them there.

Liz fell back down on the couch and shook her head. There wasn't anything to do about it. Without talking to Chad, she didn't know what else to think. They were most likely sleeping together. At least a 95% probability. Yet, even if there was only a 75% probability, why even indulge in thoughts about him? And who knew when he would be back to Chicago again and able to discuss with her all the reasons she should believe him? Besides, why should she buy anything he ever told her again?

Liz groaned and stood up from the couch. There she was, still thinking about him. "What good is that going to do? He betrayed my trust by having another woman in his hotel room. And to call her babe? Why? Who is she?"

Liz shook her head. "Stop torturing yourself!" She leaned against the couch and closed her eyes. It was all going to somehow work itself out. She only wished she knew when that would be.

Her phone started ringing, and she quickly grabbed it, half expecting Chad's name to flash across the screen. Instead, it was Marisa. Instantly the kiss came flooding back into her mind and she couldn't stop herself from answering.

"Hello?"

"Uh, hey, Liz," Marisa started. "Wasn't sure if you would answer."

Neither was Liz. There was a greater part of her that was surprised by the way she had quickly picked up Marisa's call. Yet, in that moment, she couldn't get the images out of her mind how Chad was enjoying himself in France and Liz was stuck having to think about what it was he was doing. But her kiss still played in her mind, making her unsure how she could continue to avoid Marisa.

"Yeah, sorry I rushed off like I did earlier."

"Oh, that's okay. I get it. I mean, it's understandable with the way things ended and all at the restaurant. You know…" Marisa released a breath, and Liz could hear it echoing through the phone. "Now I'm rambling, and I promise I did have a reason to call you. I have something to tell you. Do you have a few moments?"

"Sure," Liz responded, sitting back down on the couch. After the blow from hearing that woman's voice, she wasn't going anywhere, and she could take any distraction. "What's up?"

If Marisa mentioned the kiss, that might send Liz into full-blown panic, but they would have to face it eventually. So, why not the present?

"Have you heard any news about Donovan?"

Liz's heart pounded. What was it that Marisa knew? Her

tone sounded concerned—overly concerned, even. "No, not lately, anyway. What's happened? Is he all right?"

"Oh, yeah. Right now he's fine. I don't want you to be concerned or anything. Just wanted to see if you knew the update. That's all."

"Oh, okay." Liz sighed and leaned back in her seat. Unfortunately, she had gotten too engrossed in other issues, and she hadn't visited Donovan as often as she had wanted to. "I haven't seen him in a few days."

"I had to do labs on him earlier today. I was curious, so I inquired with the staff, and they said they feel he'll benefit more at another facility. They're transferring him to Tennessee."

Liz released a breath. It wasn't horrible news, because at least this meant they were working to get him the best help they could for him. That was great. But there was a hole in the pit of her stomach. Once Donovan was out of the hospital, she would lose all contact with him. She hadn't had enough time getting to know the kid, and for that, she was sad.

"I'm happy if he can get the help he deserves—the help he needs. But, sure I'm sad. That's just my selfish side. I don't know what I'll do without him around."

"I just wanted to make you aware. In case you weren't."

"Thank you," Liz quietly replied.

She wasn't yet ready to end the call. Marisa's voice was too comforting. "So, um, what are you up to?"

She didn't want to be there, in her home, alone and think about her missing ring. She didn't want to have to think about her failing engagement. She just needed someone. Anyone.

Don't lie to yourself, Liz. You know Marisa is the one you need.

"Probably wine and Netflix. My typical weekend night."

Liz swallowed, almost too shy to ask. "Well, I have both wine and Netflix. If you want to come over."

There was a long pause on the other end of the line, so long that Liz had to rest her hand from holding the phone. She shook her hand out, waiting for her reply.

"I don't know," Marisa started.

"If I'm being honest, I think that I need us to talk about what happened between us—clear the air and all that stuff. I enjoy being around you Marisa, and I don't want that to end."

Plus, I just need to figure out this stuff happening in my life right now.

Liz sighed. "Look, there are just some things I think we need to talk about. That's all."

"See you in fifteen," Marisa replied softly.

When Liz hung up, she knew having a talk with Marisa was the right thing to do. And clearing the air with her about Chad would finally have everything out in the open. What she didn't account for was that the mere thought of telling Marisa about Chad would go out the window fifteen minutes later, when she showed up.

"There's wine chilling in the fridge and Netflix already on. Go pick a show and I'll be right out."

Liz grabbed two glasses, the bottle of wine, and a corkscrew, then carried it all out into the living room, where Marisa was relaxing on the couch and staring at the television screen.

"Did you find us a show?" Liz asked, placing the glasses on the coffee table.

Marisa looked up and shrugged. "Don't really feel like Netflix." She shrugged again and looked over to the glass.

"Wine, on the other hand…" She picked her glass up and looked up to meet Liz's gaze. "Yes, please."

Liz tilted her head. She was confused as to why Netflix didn't much appeal to Marisa, despite that it the one thing—well, one out of two, including the wine—Marisa said she wanted to do that night. She put in the corkscrew and started to turn it, then popped the cork out and poured Marisa a glass.

"Thank you!" Marisa replied, taking a drink before Liz could pour her own glass.

"It's good, I hope," Liz replied, putting down the glass. "Didn't even get in a toast."

Marisa laughed, taking the glass away from her lips and nodding. "Just what I needed. Now, if you want to say a toast, go for it."

Liz looked down at her glass, then sat down on the spot next to Marisa. She looked over to Marisa, who now held a curious stare. Nerves suddenly shot to Liz's stomach. What kind of toast could she make? *New friendships? Old relationships coming to a screeching halt?*

She raised her glass and met Marisa's stare. "Here's to people getting to know each other and overcoming obstacles, and to finding one's purpose."

Marisa arched an eyebrow. "I'll drink to that. And to being honest with yourself and others."

She tossed her head back as she downed half her glass. Liz watched her, curious by that last statement. When Marisa finished her drink, she turned to Liz and Liz quickly took a sip.

And to finding out what Marisa meant.

She put her glass down on a coaster, then slid another coaster over to Marisa.

Marisa laughed.

"What?" Liz asked.

"I don't know. That was just a mature thing to do. Heck, I don't even know that I could find my coasters." She smirked as she put her glass down on the offered coaster.

"So, you're calling me old?" Liz teased.

Marisa held up a hand. "Not old, mature. It isn't often that someone of your age would even think about using a coaster."

"Probably something my mom instilled in my brain." Liz laughed as she picked her glass up and took a sip. "I would say that has something to do with one's upbringing."

"Yeah, I suppose you're right," Marisa replied.

The living room turned quiet, and Liz looked over to the television, the Netflix home screen still pulled up. She grabbed the remote and turned the TV off, then put it back in its basket.

"There's something I need to tell you." Marisa's words came out in a rush as Liz turned back to her.

Liz opened her mouth, but Marisa held out her hand and touched her arm. "Let me get this out there before I lose my nerve."

Liz nodded.

"So, I like you, Liz. I have tried to push those feelings aside because you're so much younger than me. But the truth is, it's becoming impossible. When I kissed you, it was out of instinct. I wanted to know what it would be like to feel your lips on mine."

Liz's cheeks filled with heat, but she didn't interject. Hearing Marisa's words left her feeling something inside of her that she thought was dead. It was something she hadn't felt in a long time, even with Chad. She felt renewed hope that maybe something more was out there for her. She felt even excitement that welled up inside of her.

"The age difference is something that I feel is too hard to get past, but then when you do something like the coaster thing, I think maybe I'm just being crazy or even maybe I'm the immature one."

Liz tilted her head. "So, just the mere act of using a coaster has you thinking that, oh, maybe I'm not so young after all?"

"Look at me, Liz."

Liz slowly turned to look in Marisa's direction. Liz's breath hitched as she stared at her, not sure if she should continue to look or force herself to look away. Her heart was in play, and she knew that if she continued staring, she would do the inevitable and kiss her.

"If I thought for one minute what I'm feeling would never be reciprocated, then I'd turn away. I'd never look back. But seeing your eyes locked on mine, and having felt your lips against mine, without one ounce of hesitancy..." Her words trailed off.

As Marisa's eyes dropped to Liz's lips, Liz sucked her bottom lip instinctively. Just the thought of Marisa kissing her again excited her and made her feel a longing that she didn't know existed. In this moment, though, there was more. Heat built up inside of her, and she couldn't pull herself away from that.

Marisa reached out and slowly grazed her hand over Liz's cheek. Liz locked eyes with her, and it was Liz who slowly moved in, capturing Marisa's lips against hers.

Hold me. I want to feel your arms around me.

The words echoed through Liz's head as she scooted in closer to Marisa.

Marisa's tongue swooped in, claiming a moan that was deep inside of Liz. Marisa said breathlessly, "Once we go there..."

Liz dropped her gaze to Marisa's, waiting for Marisa to go on.

"There's no going back."

"I wouldn't want to," Liz whispered before she crashed her lips onto Marisa's again.

She pulled herself up and straddled her legs around Marisa's waist, breaking from the kiss only long enough for Marisa to slide her hands under Liz's shirt and pull it up and over Liz's head. Liz frantically went back in for another kiss, not wanting to take a moment away from pressing against her soft lips. She felt Marisa's hand at her bra, and there wasn't any doubt this was right where she craved to be. Marisa removed her bra with a flick of the wrist, and Liz slipped out of it, her breasts touching Marisa's. She wanted nothing more than to be right there, in Marisa's arms, and seeing what their future could hold. She could worry about the aftermath later.

CHAPTER FIFTEEN

Marisa

Marisa shifted in bed and her arm wrapped around the warm and naked body beside her. She opened her eyes, smiling as the images of Liz came tumbling through her mind. With lovemaking like that, who could even fathom that age even mattered? She shifted next to Liz and turned to look at her. The cover was draped loosely over Liz's petite body. Marisa pulled back the covers and kissed the inside of Liz's cleavage, which made Liz let out a groan that only intensified the heat inside of Marisa.

Marisa tossed the cover back and moved in, splaying several kisses down Liz's body until she reached the core of Liz's femininity. Liz groaned, giving Marisa the motivation to move in. Marisa took in a whiff of Liz's scent and smiled to herself. She could definitely get used to this. No way was age going to deter her at that moment, when Liz's satisfaction was at the brink of all of Marisa's desires.

Her breath brushed against Liz's opening, a place she had spent much of the night before sleep overtook them. Before she could even caress that very spot, Liz moaned and shifted in bed.

"Marisa?" Liz whispered.

"Right here, babe," Marisa replied, shifting between Liz's legs to look up into Liz's expectant stare. Liz closed her legs and her eyes dropped. Marisa frowned at that. Was something wrong? Was Liz regretting their time spent getting to know one another intimately?

"Something wrong?" Marisa asked, pulling herself up and plopping down into the spot where she had been sleeping only minutes earlier.

Liz glanced over at Marisa and her face looked as white as the sheet that was on her bed.

"You regret it." Marisa quickly looked away. "That's fine. I should have known it was possible. I mean, this is all new to you. You were simply exploring. No need to say anything." She tossed the covers to the side and slipped out of bed. "I'll just find my clothes and get out of here."

"Marisa, will you hold up for a minute?" Liz reached out and trailed her finger down Marisa's arm. Before her hand could reach Marisa's, Marisa pulled back.

She shook her head. "It's easiest if I just go. No one needs to feel awkward. It is what it is. Happens all the time."

Liz pulled her hand back and her eyebrows furrowed into a straight line. Marisa tossed a look to Liz, who nodded. "Happens all the time? Okay, then. Must've been no big deal to you."

Marisa's jaw dropped, pain resounding inside of her when she heard those words. She slowly backed away from the bed, tripping over her shoe as she tried to reach the door. Tears stung her eyes, and that infuriated her because she was supposed to be the regal one, the one mature who didn't let some simple statement rattle her. Yet, there was a lump in her throat and her vision was blurred.

Do not let her see you like this.

Marisa spun on her heel and grabbed the shoe from the floor, then picked up her panties and bra, hurrying to get out of there. When she reached the door, she turned around to face Liz, her jaw clenched. Before she could leave, she had to get this out there or she was liable never to have the chance.

"Is that what you think?" Marisa asked. She pulled on her bra and brought her panties back up, still gawking at Liz over on the bed. "You think that it meant nothing and that I'm just flippant about what happened between us? If that's so, then you don't know me at all."

Her breath hitched, and she mentally cursed herself for showing her pain to Liz. She turned around and said, "It's fine and all, but that's not how I feel," before leaving.

"Marisa. Wait!" Liz called out before Marisa could get to the stairs. Before Marisa stepped onto the top stair, she felt Liz's hand on her shoulder. When she looked over at her, Liz's face softened. She now was in just a T-shirt.

"I'm sorry if I offended you. It's just, it seemed like you were saying it was no big deal that we had sex. Not just once, but multiple times. I guess I was protecting my feelings."

"You were protecting yours?" Marisa turned and faced her. "I was protecting mine. You were filled with regret, and I didn't want you to think that it was breaking me down inside. But the truth is…" Marisa swallowed the lump that had never left her throat. "It was."

"If you saw regret in my eyes, I can't deny that."

"Great! A fantastic way of boosting my ego. Thanks a lot."

Marisa looked away from Liz. She wanted to bolt, get out of there and never look back, but something kept holding her steadfast to the top of those stairs.

"It's not what you think, though. Please…Come back into the bedroom so we can talk. I'm begging you."

Before Marisa knew it, Liz grabbed her hand and was pulling her back through the bedroom doorway. Liz sat down on the edge of the bed and tried to pull Marisa down to the spot beside her, but Marisa leaned against the dresser.

"I'm good here," Marisa mumbled.

"Suit yourself," Liz softly replied. Marisa met Liz's gaze and Liz's eyes went dark before she looked down at her hands. There was something she was hiding. Marisa could sense that from even all the way across the room. She was fidgety, and when she looked up, a tear trickled down her cheek.

"I haven't been honest with you," Liz whispered.

Marisa didn't even attempt to reply. She just watched her. Waiting. Waiting for whatever it was that Liz felt she had to get off her chest. The waiting was slowly killing her inside, but Marisa didn't move. She just waited.

"I don't know that you'll ever forgive me."

"Just tell me," Marisa stated.

Her words pleaded for Liz to go on. Nothing could be that hard, right? Yet, there was so much angst and anxiety in Liz's eyes that Marisa worried she was wrong on so many levels. "I don't know that I can wait another minute, or even second. What's going on here?"

"I'm engaged to be married, Marisa," Liz yelled out.

The blood drained from Marisa's cheeks as Liz slid down the bed and brought herself to her heels. She had to have heard her wrong. This was some kind of joke. It was the only explanation she could focus on. Please, someone tell her this was some big mistake and Liz didn't just utter those words. Liz didn't move to explain herself and Marisa knew that she wasn't dreaming. Her world had just come crashing down around her.

CHAPTER SIXTEEN

Liz

From across the bedroom, Marisa stared at her bottle of water. Somehow, the two had switched places: she was now sitting on the bed and Liz was standing across the room. Liz opened her mouth to say something, but then slowly shut it again. She was relieved Marisa hadn't bolted out of there the minute she dropped the bombshell. She hadn't meant it to come out like that, but it seemed like she couldn't stop the words from sounding the way they did. Marisa needed to know. But like this? She wasn't so sure that had been the way to go. She nibbled on her lower lip and waited for Marisa to do something.

As if in response, Marisa lifted the bottle to her lips and took a swig. Not quite the action Liz had wanted.

"Are you going to say something?" Liz asked.

Marisa snickered. "I don't know what you want me to say,

Liz. You're getting married. I just had sex with someone who is about to walk down the aisle. Yay me."

She took another drink and her eyes dropped to the top of the bottle. Liz's chest caved, and she wanted to rush over there and pull Marisa into her arms. Still, she continued standing.

"It isn't like that," Liz started, wanting to scream at herself. How could she have done this to the one person she'd connected with? It was hard to fathom that she could actually be forgiven. "It wasn't like this was on a whim."

"Oh? It wasn't?" Marisa looked up, her eyebrow arching. "Explain that to me, because from where I'm sitting, it looks exactly like that. It looks like you were set to see where things could go, not thinking about anyone else's feelings. Not thinking about how it would affect me. Isn't that right?"

"No," Liz blurted out. "Will you please let me just explain my side of things? Please."

She pleaded with her because the thought of Marisa running away from her at that point would only bring Liz back to the state she was in when she first heard the woman on the other end of the line.

Marisa glared at Liz, finally giving her the attention Liz had asked for. It was now or never. "Yes, I'm engaged. I'm engaged to a man. I won't try to deny that."

"You really can't. You just blurted that out to me fifteen minutes earlier."

Marisa glowered at Liz and Liz slowly nodded. Marisa tossed her head back, downing the rest of her water.

"It's in name only," she said.

Marisa frowned, but Liz quickly explained. "Chad is someone my mother pushed for. My parents would have had me married five years ago if they had their way. Chad was the guy who could give me what I wanted. Or, rather, what they wanted me to have. Sure, I looked for a relationship that would reflect the one I saw in my parents, but it was Chad that my parents wanted for me. When he proposed, I honestly thought I had no other choice."

Marisa sighed and stood up from the bed. "You really don't need to explain yourself. If I was some last-minute fling that you wanted to see if you were ready to commit to your fiancé, then so be it."

"Listen to me, Marisa. Please. Because that's not it at all."

Liz pushed herself off the wall and started to move toward Marisa. Marisa crossed her arms and dropped her eyes to the floor before sitting back down on the bed. It was a defensive way of pushing Liz away and Liz understood that. Liz turned and walked over to a chair, then sunk down into it.

"I didn't plan this, thinking that I would hook up with a woman and try to see what I was missing. You just happened to be there. I'm sorry that was the way it happened, but I don't regret it."

Marisa looked up, her gaze landing on Liz's. "Then why? Why me?"

Liz shook her head. "I planned on telling you at the restaurant, but then the timing just never seemed to be right. I even brought my engagement ring to tell you everything, but we got to talking and I realized that telling you could mean losing your friendship. I had spent so much time hiding this that I didn't want you to think I didn't know to be truthful."

Marisa smirked. "So, you didn't want me to see how you truly are. Is that it?"

Liz dropped her gaze. She felt a tear slowly sneaking up on her and she willed it to go away.

"That came out all wrong," Marisa softly stated.

Liz shook her head. "No. It's understandable. I let the kiss linger when I should have stopped it right there. Then tonight was unthinkable. I allowed us to have sex all while knowing this truth. But, you see, before you called, I realized that I had lost my engagement ring. Somehow it had fallen out of my purse, and I called Chad to tell him what happened. Then I realized he's not on a business trip alone. He's with another woman. I was feeling lonely, and it's not some horrid excuse, but it's the truth. I was lonely. You called, and all I thought was how I needed to see you. How I wanted to see you. You were in the right place at the wrong time, but Marisa, I needed that."

Marisa's eyes softened, and Liz had a brief glimmer of hope, of Marisa walking over to her and pulling her into her arms, telling her everything would be okay, and possibly kissing her to comfort her. She held onto that feeling, but Marisa's eyes hardened, and she scoffed.

"What bothers me the most is at the time, I planned on throwing caution to the wind and saying screw all the fears about age and who cares about anything that might have divided us. I let my guard down. I allowed myself to open myself up to feeling this way. I allowed myself to let go and just relax and then this happens. I can't even say I regret that because it *was* time for me to open myself up to feelings like this. And I needed that. I regret that you're not available, but it is what it is."

"But I am," Liz argued. "My engagement is over, as far as I'm concerned."

Marisa's eyebrows furrowed, and she stood up from the bed. "But you're not. You're not free and I'm not going to be the other woman. I deserve more than that. And as the mature one in this duo, I have to walk away."

Liz swallowed the lump that had formed in her throat. "I'm sorry if I hurt you."

Liz stood up as Marisa started to move past her. Marisa reached out and touched Liz's shoulder.

"Don't be sorry. Goodbye, Liz."

She walked past Liz and Liz turned to watch her leave. She opened her mouth to plead with her to stay, but as she walked away, she knew that it was right to let her go. She fell into the chair and felt her heart aching as Marisa closed the door. She waited a second before she jumped up, hurried out the door, and ran down the stairs. By the time she got the door open to run out and beg Marisa to stay, she saw her backing out of the driveway. It was too late, and Marisa was heading further away from her.

Liz turned and went back into the house. She fell back against the door as she closed it behind her. Her phone started ringing, and Liz thought that maybe Marisa was calling her. When she reached the table where her phone lay face down, she grabbed it and spotted Chad's name. Her heart fell as she answered the call.

"Hello? Chad?"

"Hey, babe," he started. "Funny thing, I left my phone at a board meeting and just got it back. One of the women there said she answered your call. Gosh, babe, I miss you."

Another lie. Liz sat down on the couch, her heart racing from her conversation with Marisa a few moments earlier. Right now wasn't the time or place to get into it with Chad, but that moment would come. She was getting stronger to finally have that conversation.

Liz walked up to the desk and Mindi looked up and smiled. "Hey, Mindi!"

She nodded. "Hey, it's been a few days."

Liz nodded. "Too long. Just came to see the little man. Hear he might be headed off to Tennessee soon."

She started to walk past the desk and toward Donovan's room.

"No one called you?" Mindi asked, bringing Liz's attention back to the front desk. "Thought Victoria might reach out or something."

"What do you mean? I haven't heard anything, outside Donovan going to Tennessee."

Mindi shrugged. "Guess they thought it would be better to have a clean break. But he's already gone. They had a clinical trial opening, and he needed to be there today."

Mindi's phone rang, and she grabbed it across the desk as Liz stared at her, tears already threatening to fall. He was already gone? How'd this happen? Why didn't someone call her? She looked away from the desk and her breath hitched. If she hadn't talked to Marisa, she wouldn't have even known that he was leaving the hospital. At least she was forewarned. She turned away when she heard her name.

"He did write you this letter."

She reached out as Mindi handed her the letter.

"Thank you," Liz mumbled. It wasn't the same. Liz tucked it into her pocket, not wanting to read it until she had some privacy. She was off for the day, and she found herself heading out to the garden. It was the last place she had been with Donovan—just the two of them. She now considered it their place. She was relieved to see she was out there alone and sat down on one of the benches. When she opened it, she braced herself; she knew the note would make her emotional.

Dear Liz —

I want to thank you. Thank you for being you. I have enjoyed our time together, no matter how short it might have been. Know that you have helped me. You have helped my mom, too. I will never forget you. And whatever happens to me, know that you have been a smile that I've loved. So, thank you! You are my sunshine, Liz. I hope that I've been yours.

Love,
Donovan

Liz wiped the tears that had fallen down her cheeks as she folded the note and put it back into her pocket. Donovan was a strong boy, and she wanted to be just as strong for him. She stood up from the bench and turned to head back into the hospital.

Marisa walked out of the hospital and Liz spotted her first.

When Marisa's gaze went to hers, Liz wiped the tears away and opened her mouth to say something. It would come out all wrong, she knew. But she didn't even get the chance to. Marisa turned on her heel and hurried back into the hospital.

Liz looked down at the ground, steadying herself and hoping she didn't fall to her knees. Life was turning out way too hard and she couldn't stand there and watch everything fall apart around her. She grabbed her phone from her pocket and closed her eyes, anxious for the tears to stay away.

A voice answered the call after the first ring. "Hello?"

"Hey, Mom," Liz spoke, the tears thick in her throat.

"Liz? Are you crying?"

Liz released a forced giggle. "Of course not. Just wanted to let you know that I'm coming for a few days to visit."

Her mom squealed into the phone and Liz pulled the phone away from her ear. At least her mom sounded excited to have her there.

"What's the occasion? Are you coming to start working on the prep for the wedding?"

The excitement laced through her mom's voice was like a dagger to Liz's chest. She could already see the disappointment on her parents' faces when she told them the wedding wasn't going to happen. Then again, she still needed to tell Chad that. But first things first, she needed a break from the hospital and a break from reality.

"Nah, just wanted to see you guys. That's all. Any problem with that? I can get a few days off work and no better time than the present. Might as well, right?"

"Of course, honey. And that doesn't have to stop us from talking about wedding plans. I'm so excited to see you."

"Yeah, I'm looking forward to it, too."

She collapsed against the building, prepared to break down in tears. She bit down on her lower lip and heaved a sigh. "I have to go, but I'll be heading to Indy in the morning."

"Sounds good. I'll prepare your old bedroom."

Liz smiled. "Love you, Mom."

"Love you, too."

Liz quickly hung up the call and stayed there for a moment. She felt like she was running around. In a sense, maybe she was, but her heart ached that she now didn't even have Marisa to talk to.

Can you blame her? You had sex and then said, "Oh and by the way, I'm getting married."

Liz covered her face and shook her head. She would be devastated, too, if she was Marisa. It was awful that she had played with her heart in a way that she couldn't ignore.

Liz entered the hospital and took the elevator to the ER floor. Sally sat behind the computer and stared absentmindedly at it. She yawned, covering her mouth, then looked up and met Liz's gaze. She smiled as she pulled her hand away.

"I didn't know you were still here," Sally said.

"You look exhausted."

Sally nodded. "Rough day already."

Liz looked around the empty waiting room. At least Sally had a break in action at that moment. "Just about to head out, but I have a question. How do I put in a request for some time off?"

Sally arched an eyebrow. "For how long?"

Liz shrugged. "A few days maybe. Some things are going on at home and I really could use some time away. I know that puts everyone in a bind, but I don't see a way out of it. Whom should I speak with?"

"Frank, I'd say." Sally smiled. "There's a lot of us looking for work, so I doubt it will matter. But I saw him headed to his office. He's probably still here."

"Thanks!" Liz turned, but Sally's voice made her jerk her head to look over her shoulder.

"I hope everything is okay. I know all too well about family drama. I'll be thinking of you." She got up from her desk and gave a genuine smile.

"Thanks, Sally." Liz turned and headed straight for his office. Things would be fine if she took just a few moments to herself. She had to get away from thoughts of Chad and her feelings for Marisa. It was the only way she would be able to clear her head and figure out where her heart really belonged.

CHAPTER SEVENTEEN

Marisa

The computer screen blurred as Marisa stared at it, the words suddenly losing focus. She looked down and covered her eyes. Had the day been that long that she couldn't even focus on what was right in front of her? No, she knew the truth. She just couldn't get her mind off the woman down in the ER. Marisa opened her eyes and stared at the screen once more. If she kept this up, she would be forced to end her shift and head home.

She had a couple more hours to get through. Then she could drown her sorrows in as much alcohol as she wanted. Forget the Netflix; it would be alcohol, her tears, and her bedroom. It'd been three days since she'd last seen Liz out in the garden and she still pictured the way Liz had looked. Her eyes were red. She was crying. But for what? Her? She didn't want her to look so down and out. Marisa turned and looked away from the computer as the other monitor dinged a notification that her next patient was there.

"Perfect timing," she groaned. Now if she could just keep her tears at bay, she would be able to get through the next couple of hours. Marisa stood up and went to the cabinets to pull out the vials for her patient's labs.

Once she had her work area ready, she left the back room and went out to the front. Samantha sat behind the computer and looked over to meet Marisa's stare. Marisa gave her a weak grin. Since they had their last conversation about how Marisa didn't feel the same way Samantha did, they had kept their relationship strictly professional. It wasn't fair to Samantha when it might only confuse the situation. Yet, Samantha usually smiled at her in passing, so maybe she had moved on and realized it was a frivolous attempt when Marisa gave no sign that she felt the same.

"Lucile?" Marisa called out, turning her eyes back to the waiting room. The only woman there got up and walked over to greet Marisa. "I'm Marisa and I'll be drawing your labs today. How are you doing?"

"Nervous," the older woman said. She smiled, but her eyes seemed droopy. "Don't like getting my blood drawn."

Marisa smiled. "I've got you. We'll get through this together." It was what she needed to get Liz out of her mind and focus her attention on the woman who needed her attention and support right now.

Marisa talked to Lucile softly as she prepared the woman's arm to get her blood drawn. She kept the conversation going while she drew the four vials of blood, then pulled the tourniquet off as the woman looked up.

"You're all set," Marisa said.

The woman's jaw dropped. "Really?"

Marisa nodded. "Your doctor will have your results within two days. Enjoy the rest of your day."

The woman clapped her hands together. "That was the best blood draw I've ever had."

Marisa nodded. She liked to hear that. She waved to the woman and carried the paper to the computer to finalize her portion and get the labs ready to be processed. She heard the door open as she finished putting the last vial in the envelope for it to go out through the mail.

"She seemed happier than when she got here," Samantha said, leaning against Marisa's desk.

Marisa snickered. "That's my job, right?"

Samantha nodded. She didn't move to leave, so Marisa looked back over at her.

"So, can we talk?" Samantha asked.

"Don't you have patients to triage?"

"Don't have any scheduled for almost an hour. I think I'll be fine, and it won't take long. But I feel like I owe it to myself to say something."

Marisa nodded. There it was. They were going to be forced to have an awkward conversation, and she wasn't prepared for that. She closed the envelope and looked up. "You gonna make this all cringeworthy and awkward?"

Samantha scrunched up her nose, then laughed and shook her head. "Not unless you want me to. Honestly, I was going to say that I get why things wouldn't work out with us. I mean, we work so closely together and I'm much younger than you. I can think of a million reasons why you and I wouldn't work out. Not to mention, I'm not sure I'm really a lesbian. Or, maybe I am, but you probably don't want someone to experiment on you. I get it."

Marisa quickly looked away. Samantha had literally described things between her and Liz. Coming from an outsider's perspective, Marisa figured that maybe she was only trying to have something that would never have worked out. It was disheartening, but then maybe it was good for her that Liz wound up being engaged.

You don't buy that for a minute. Marisa sunk down in her chair. She couldn't fool herself, so why try to fool anyone else. She looked up and Samantha smirked.

"You want to know the main reason I know you and I wouldn't work out?"

"I'm all ears," Marisa mumbled.

"Because you've got it bad for someone else. I couldn't compete with that. And I realize this. So, yeah, it's troubling to have to take myself down a few notches, but it's really the only thing that can happen. What's confusing is the fact that you're all about the age difference and I'm literally just a couple years younger than her, so yeah, that hurts a bit. But, hey, you just aren't into me in that way. It is what it is. But I can see there's been a change and I'm thinking maybe she's also shown you that she likes you. So, this is no longer a one-way street."

Her infectious smile lit up the room and Marisa sighed with relief.

"Wanna talk about it?" Samantha asked.

Marisa smirked and looked away from her. "So, it's that

obvious, huh?" She looked back as Samantha stepped back and leaned against the wall.

"It wasn't. Or, maybe I was just trying to ignore it. But there's been a sudden shift in how you're holding yourself, and I saw how you would light up whenever Liz was around. It would take a blind person not to see that. What I worried about was the fact that Liz is definitely not a lesbian, and she didn't look like someone that would swing your way." She held out her hand and quirked up an eyebrow. "No offense."

"None taken. And I get it. I thought that, too. But then…" Her words drifted off and an image of Liz's naked body pressed into the back of her mind. She shuddered, wanting that image to dissipate. "It just would never work out."

"Well, that look on your face tells me otherwise," Samantha quietly replied. "So, I'm guessing that you attempted it."

"We attempted it," Marisa mumbled. "Then everything fell apart. Because what she had failed to mention to me was that she's engaged. To a guy. So, there is nothing that points to us working out in any sensible fashion." She shrugged. "So be it."

"You wanna know what attracted me to you in the first place?"

Marisa scrunched up her nose and Samantha laughed. "Don't worry. It has nothing to do with your looks."

Marisa felt her cheeks burning. Was it smart to have this conversation? Not really, but she wasn't going to turn from it. Not when Samantha seemed invested in getting her point across to her.

"It's the fact that you're so confident about everything. You carry yourself in a way that makes anybody feel like they can do anything they set their mind to. And I believed that. That's sexy to me. Even more than looks can be."

Marisa blushed, focusing her attention back on her computer screen. Samantha wasn't through talking. "You don't find that in too many people. I know for certain that I don't have that. I was drawn to your self-confidence, and I was drawn to your maturity. So, it bothers me that you're just giving up."

"I'm not giving up," Marisa argued. "But how can I compete with a guy that she's known a lot longer and agreed to marry him?"

"Have you asked her that? Is she happy?"

Marisa looked up. Was that important? Liz hadn't been honest with her. That was what she couldn't get past. Yet, Marisa didn't know whether she had been able to give her the chance to be honest with her. If she was hiding her fiancé, then clearly she felt she had a reason to. Was that enough, though?

"You're pretty smart for being a young'un."

Samantha laughed. "Maybe I'll find someone as mature as you are someday. But I know that if you want something or someone, you need to try to make it work. Fight for what's important to you. It's the only thing you should want to do. Do you think Liz is worth that?"

Marisa didn't hesitate as she nodded.

"Then you know what you need to do."

Marisa looked down at her envelope with the vial of blood. "Can you handle it up here for fifteen minutes?" Marisa asked.

"I'll manage," Samantha said.

Marisa grabbed her phone and the envelopes meant for the mail slot and hurried out of the office. The moment she got in the elevator, she called Liz.

"Hi, you've reached Liz," Liz's voice stated, going straight to voicemail.

Marisa pushed the button for the main floor and stared at the numbers as they slowly descended. It was best not to dwell on what she would say and just blurt it out once she got there. Finally, the door opened, and she rushed into the ER. She slowed her pace as she walked straight to the desk. Hanna sat behind the desk at one end and looked up when Marisa approached her.

"Hey, I can see you're busy," Marisa started.

Hanna nodded. "It's been a crazy day and we're short-staffed and…" She sighed. "Don't want to get into all of that. Do you need something?"

"Um." Marisa looked around the waiting room and her eyes trailed down the main hallway. Things were still different with Hanna because Hanna didn't understand Marisa and her attempt to be friends with Liz. Now Marisa wondered if that was because she knew about Liz's fiancé.

Hanna cleared her throat, bringing Marisa's gaze to her.

"Is Liz working?" she blurted out.

Hanna sighed. "I wish, but she took off a few days. A few usually means three, right? Well, it's been three days and not a word. So, who really knows? It's some family business, apparently. Gotta get back to work, but if you hear from her, be sure to let her know we're anxious for her to come back."

Hanna rushed off and Marisa gawked at the front desk. She was gone? Gone where? Family business? She turned and headed to the elevator, then looked at the envelope in her hand. She took a detour down another hallway to the mailroom. When she entered, she was alone.

She looked over to the mail slots and saw that Liz's slot was jammed full of papers. She frowned, confused. Maybe she had rushed off to be with her fiancé. Nothing would have surprised her at that moment.

She dropped the vial into the mail slot for the outgoing mail and looked over to the door. She walked over to Liz's slot and started to reach for her mail, but quickly pulled back her hand. What would rifling through Liz's mail even change? It wouldn't explain where she was or why she had left.

She left the mailroom with just her own mail in her hand. She took the nearest elevator back to the lab. The moment she stepped into the lab, Samantha looked up.

"That was fast," she said.

Marisa shrugged. "Apparently everything I thought I knew is no more. Liz didn't even care enough to tell me she was taking some time off." Samantha opened her mouth, but Marisa shook her head. "Don't want to talk about it."

She shut the door behind her and slumped down in the nearest chair. Things would never be able to go back to the way they were. Not now. Not ever.

MARISA WALKED UP TO SAMANTHA AS SHE LOGGED ONTO HER computer. She looked over and gave Marisa a tentative smile.

Marisa shrugged. "I'm not going to break. I've been through a lot more heartache than this right here. It just wasn't meant to be."

"Great! Glad you're feeling so positive over it."

Marisa smirked. Positive wasn't exactly the right word to

use for it. She had been upset over the past two days since finding out about Liz, but it was what it was and she wasn't going to think about it. If she did, then it was likely that she would crawl into a hole and never want to leave. What good would that do?

"Wanna go grab some coffee?" Samantha asked.

"How about beer?" Marisa asked, grinning.

Samantha laughed and shrugged. "Whichever. I'm game."

"Great! Let's get out of here."

"Do you work tomorrow?" Samantha asked as they left the lab and Marisa locked up behind them.

"Nope. I might sleep the day away," Marisa teased.

"Me too, girlfriend."

Samantha laughed and Marisa put a genuine smile on her face. Before this drama had happened, she could see herself hanging with Samantha as a friend, so maybe that was where this would bring them. Since things weren't awkward between them, it was at least a start. The door of the elevator opened, and they saw Sally standing in the elevator.

She let out a sigh as she got off the elevator. "I'm relieved you're still here," she said.

"You have a patient?" Marisa asked. She tossed a look over to Samantha. "Might have to take a raincheck." She turned back to Sally.

Sally shook her head. "No, but Liz is probably going to kill me."

Marisa frowned. "Liz?"

From the corner of Marisa's eye, she saw Samantha quirk up an eyebrow.

Sally held out a piece of paper that was folded into four

squares. Marisa took it from her and saw her name scrawled on the side of it.

"I didn't read it," Sally said quickly. "But she asked me to give it to you and then I forgot and then I lost it." She shook her head. "My head has seriously been a mess lately. I'm really sorry about that. If you could please try to protect me, I'd appreciate it."

"No problem," Marisa said, still looking at her name, carefully written across the paper. "Thanks, Sally."

Sally turned and got back in the elevator. "Are you going down?" she asked.

Marisa looked up as Samantha got onto the elevator. Samantha smiled softly and nodded. "I am. You on the other hand...Have a good weekend, Marisa."

Marisa waved and then looked back at the note as she carefully opened it.

Dearest Marisa —

I don't know where to start. The truth is, I've literally started this note a hundred times and every time I get to the end I throw it away. What it boils down to is I can't think of what to say to you because there's so much I want to say. I know that sounds so cliché and maybe it is, but what isn't cliché is how I feel about you. I didn't expect it. I didn't anticipate it. And I certainly didn't look for it. I didn't know what I was looking for, but I knew I was always looking for something to put my heart back together. It was you all along and I didn't even know it.

Yes, I'm engaged. Am I happy? No! Truth is, I haven't been happy for a long time. When I talk to you, that's me at my happiest. Why would I run from that? Because I'm scared, that's why. I should have been honest with you. You are the one person I have in my life I feel I should always be honest with. I don't have that feeling for Chad and that also scares me.

Do I have things to work out? Heck yeah, I have things to work out. I don't know where I can take this or even if you'll ever forgive me to make things right with you. I wouldn't blame you if you never wanted to see me again. But I beg you to at least give me the opportunity to tell you how truly sorry I am. If you have read the letter up to this point, I feel I have some chance.

As I'm sure you have already figured out, I've taken some time away. I needed that, and I went to my parents' house in Indianapolis. It might just be the break I need. But I won't be gone long and I hope that we can talk things through.

Please just forgive me. I need to know I haven't screwed things up so much that I've permanently messed things up between us.

When I get back, I will know exactly what's in my heart. But I can tell you what I feel now and it's every kiss we have shared. It's the warmth you bring to my body when I think about you. And it's every smile you bring to my face. Am I getting cheesy? Probably. But just thinking about being with you brings me the warmth and desire I need in my life.

I look forward to having some deep conversations with you.

Sincerely,
Liz

Marisa stared at the heart that followed Liz's name and she couldn't keep the smile from trailing her lips. She held the letter to her chest and closed her eyes. It was everything she would have said to her if given the chance. She thought Liz was running from her. She was upset that she didn't get the opportunity to talk to her because she was already gone. But soon. Very soon. She just might get that happiness after all.

CHAPTER EIGHTEEN

Liz

A knock sounded on the bedroom door. Liz groaned and tossed her legs over the side of the bed, pulling herself into a seated position. "Yeah?" she called out.

Her mother peeked her head into the room. "Are you hungry? I made soup and sandwiches."

Liz shrugged. "Not really."

Her mother frowned, coming further into the room. "Are you sure? You've been here a week and have hardly eaten anything. I'm worried about you. Something isn't right. Are you still up for wedding dress shopping?"

No!

Liz looked up and met her mom's gaze. "If I say no, can we put it off?"

That brought a frown to her mother's face. "I don't understand. You've done virtually no planning on this wedding. Are you going just to stay engaged forever?"

Liz's phone rang, and she anxiously reached across the bed and grabbed it. She frowned as she saw Chad's name. She had been waiting for—even expected—a call from Marisa. The last thing she wanted to do was hash over what she had to talk to Chad about. She slid the button on her screen to ignore the call and tossed her phone to the side.

"Did you and Chad have a fight?" her mother asked.

Liz looked up and gawked at her mother. "To fight would mean that we've talked. We don't talk, Mother. If you took the time to actually see what I wanted, then you would realize that."

Her mother's eyes bugged out, and Liz sighed. "I'm sorry. I shouldn't have spoken to you like that. No, we didn't have a fight per se. But, Mom…"

She covered her face, fearing the tears that she had tried to keep hidden for as long as she could would finally fall. When her mother sat down beside her, she leaned her head against her shoulder.

"I don't mean to be so emotional. It's just that…" She wiped her face and shook her head. "Forget I said anything."

"I can't do that," her mother said, sitting down beside her. "What's going on? You're scaring me."

Liz felt the weight on her shoulders as she stared at her mom, desperate to get it off her chest yet scared that her mother would try to tell her that she was being paranoid, that the thoughts that maybe Chad really was having an affair were all in her mind.

"There's so much going on. I don't even know where to begin," Liz poured out.

"Best to just start from the beginning. You're happy, right? With Chad?"

Liz shrugged. "I wanted to be. I've pushed to be happy. Yet, it's suddenly becoming so clear that what I thought was happiness was just me merely getting by. It's overwhelming and I feel like I can barely breathe."

"Talk to me," her mother said, reaching out and brushing her hand over Liz's shoulder.

Liz held up her hand. "Haven't you noticed I haven't been wearing the ring?"

Her mother dropped her gaze to her daughter's ring finger, then looked back at her, shocked. "Guess I really didn't."

"I lost it."

Her mother's jaw dropped, and Liz continued. "Obviously it wasn't planned. But I was out, and it came off," she lied. "I called the restaurant where I had lost it, and no one found it."

"Have you told Chad?"

"I tried," Liz mumbled. "But when I did, a woman answered the phone. He called me later and said he had left his phone at a board meeting."

"If that's what he said, then that's what happened. I'm sure of it."

Liz tilted her head and shook it. "Mom, I heard running water. His voice was in the background. He lied to me. Why? Because he's f…"

She sighed. "He's sleeping with someone else. That's blatantly obvious to me. Maybe they work together, but that doesn't change the truth."

"He wouldn't," her mother said.

Liz leaned forward, covering her face. There wasn't any

doubt that her mother would want to defend him. Both her parents already thought of him as their son. But Liz trusted her instincts.

"He isn't my one and true love. I'm sorry, but that's the truth."

She jumped up from her bed and went to the mirror. When she looked at her reflection, she saw that her eyes were red from the tears she had already cried. She turned around and noticed her mother's lips were drawn into a thin line.

"I've met someone else."

Her mom's jaw dropped. "You can't be serious. Are you saying that you're the one having an affair? Are you just trying to make yourself feel better about finding someone else?"

"Mom! No!" Liz argued. She went back to the bed and sank down on it. "I didn't plan on this. There's just something about this person that makes me think that there's no one else I'm meant to be with. And believe me, no one is more surprised than I am."

"I don't think you want to ruin your engagement, though."

Liz groaned and shook her head. "This is what you and Dad want. If you took a minute to listen to me, you would see that Chad doesn't make me happy. Chad has been in France for a month, and I've literally talked to him only a few times. What kind of engagement is that? I don't love him. It's Marisa I love."

The words came out in such a rush that Liz couldn't stop them. Once they were out there, though, she could heave a sigh. She had said it and there wasn't any going back.

Her mother's jaw dropped. "Wow. Didn't see that coming."

Her mother looked away from her and Liz prepared herself

to see her mom's heart break right in front of her. Instead, she turned and looked at her daughter.

"I don't want you to think that I don't want you to be happy. That's truly my biggest hope—that you'll find happiness and hang onto that. So, I'm surprised to hear this coming from you, but it isn't totally unexpected. Like mother like daughter, right?"

Liz frowned. "I'm confused."

"Honey, I wasn't always happy and in love with your father. It took work. The only difference is that you didn't even dare try to stay with a woman back in my day. Looking back, if I had, then you and your brother wouldn't have been here."

Liz's jaw dropped. Her mother's eyes lit up and there was a smile on her lips. "Her name was Penny. Or, is Penny, rather."

"What happened to her?"

"She's living in Houston with her husband." She smiled and reached out, stroking Liz's arm. "It was a long time ago. Just know that I know where you're coming from and if you can follow your heart, then I think you should."

"Even if it means ending things with Chad?" Liz asked.

Her mother simply nodded. "You have been here a week and I've been trying to get you to open up. I just feel that it's clear your heart or mind isn't with your fiancé."

"Are you upset?"

She shrugged. "Disappointed. But I only want you happy. Chad was your father's and my dream. That's no way to live your life."

She pulled Liz into her arms, and they embraced in a warm and loving hug. All Liz could think about was getting out of there and home to Marisa, hoping it wasn't too late to fix things.

LIZ SMILED TO HERSELF AS SHE DROVE. SHE WOULD BE HOME soon, and everything would be just as she wanted. Her phone started to ring, and she spotted Hanna's number on the line.

"Great minds," Liz replied, answering the call.

"Oh really? You were thinking of me?" Hanna asked.

"Thinking of you and Capmed."

Mostly, Marisa.

The thought left a permanent smile on her lips. "Just getting back to Chicago, so, yeah, you crossed my mind. How's work going?"

"Um, good. Busy," Hanna said. "You sound good."

"Better than I've been in a long time. It's amazing what a week can do. That's for sure. But I'm sorry you guys have been busy. I know I left you sort of stranded. My apologies for that. Just a few more days and I'll be back to work in full force."

"Um, so, yeah, there's something I need to tell you."

"Go for it," Liz replied, turning the radio down to a low murmur.

"I don't know how to tell you, but it's like this. While you were gone, it put us in a pretty big bind. And the department was forced to get someone from another department to fill in."

"Ugh. Sorry about that. Hope it wasn't too awful. A newbie?"

The ER was too difficult to have a new person filling in and Liz could already imagine the frustration in some of the nursing staff. They would hopefully get over it and be happy that she was coming back better than ever.

"No. Not really. There's a waiting list for the ER staff. Did you know that? Turns out people want the high-anxiety-type jobs. Who knew?"

Liz laughed. "Well, then it probably all worked out."

"Listen, Liz," Hanna started. "I didn't want to be the one to tell you this, but we're friends. And frankly, I would want to know if things were reversed. It's why I feel you deserve to know. You get that?"

"Uh, yeah, but what are you trying to tell me?"

Hanna sighed on the other end of the line. "They went out on a limb to hire you for the ER. They went and moved you to the top of the list. And when you weren't here, since they had to get someone else, they decided that they would replace you."

"Wow!" Liz's heart sunk a little. "So, I'm not working in the ER now. Are they putting me back in the pulmonology department? That's all right. Not the most exciting gig, but it works. It still pays. I'm not going to get upset over that. I needed to take this time away."

"I don't think you get it, Liz. Since you took the time off and it was an unexcused absence, they have decided to term you."

Liz's jaw dropped. "Seriously? You're joking, right?"

"I wish I were. And I wish I didn't have to be the one to tell you this, but again, you deserved to know. You have to be working here for longer than a year in order to have personal time like that. So, I'm sorry."

Liz shook her head, a tear hanging at the corner of her eye. If they had told her that, then maybe she wouldn't have stayed away for so long. But she thought that everything would work itself out. She might have been out of a job, but she was on her way to the house of the one person she wanted to share the news—any news, for that matter—with. There was something in that.

"Thank you for telling me, Hanna. I'm sorry I wasn't there for you guys."

"Don't say that, Liz. I'm glad you're feeling better. And you didn't let us down. We all tried to defend you. But they made up their mind."

In one week they had dropped her like she was a burden to them, so it was clear that she wasn't someone they felt they needed to protect. If that were the case, then she would have to find someone else who had her back.

"It's all right. Thanks again, Hanna. I have to go."

"Bye, Liz." Hanna's voice sounded so far away as Liz hung up. She pressed the button to call Marisa.

"H…hello?" When Marisa answered, Liz was relieved.

"I'm so glad you answered," Liz replied, a smile tugging at her lips. "Are you home? I need to see you."

"I am," Marisa replied without hesitation.

"I'll be there in five minutes. See you soon." She disconnected the call and turned down the main road that led to Marisa's house. A few minutes later she turned into Marisa's driveway. When she got up to the front door, Marisa opened the door before she could knock.

"I'm sorry," Liz said immediately. "I ran off because I was scared. I was scared that falling for you would mean losing a part of myself. What I didn't anticipate was that not being with you would bring me to the darkest places of my mind."

"You meant what was in your letter?" Marisa asked.

Liz nodded. "Every word."

Marisa reached out and grabbed Liz's hand, pulling her into

the house and closing the door behind her. Marisa kissed Liz hard, and Liz's nerves vanished completely.

"Are you ending things with Chad?" Marisa whispered, parting from the kiss.

"As soon as he's home," Liz replied.

Marisa wrapped her arms around Liz and embraced her as Liz kissed her, her tongue swooping in to claim a moan from Marisa. She wanted to stand there forever and kiss her, her heart racing, pounding, rolling like thunder in her chest. She grabbed Marisa's shirt and slowly pulled it up, over her breasts. When she was with Marisa, everything felt right, and it was time to forget her doubts and just embrace the love she felt for that woman.

CHAPTER NINETEEN

Marisa

Marisa pulled the beaded necklace from Liz's jewelry box and stared at it. Liz stepped up behind her and she felt the warmth of her lover's breath on her skin. Her body got goosebumps as Liz softly kissed Marisa's neck. Marisa tilted her head and allowed the kiss to linger. She closed her eyes and released a soft moan.

Liz snickered, pressing her lips hard enough that Marisa wouldn't have been surprised if she had left a hickey behind. "I love when you moan," Liz mumbled.

Marisa turned around, holding onto Liz's waist. "Then maybe we should just stay in. Who needs to go to the restaurant anyway, especially when we have one another?" She wrapped her arms around Liz's neck and swooped in to capture Liz's lips on hers.

"Our reservation would go to waste then, hon. We wouldn't want that, right?"

Marisa laughed. "Well, if I had my way, I would miss all the reservations if it meant getting you back in bed. You disappoint me, Liz." She winked and pulled back from the embrace. "But, if you would rather save the lovemaking for dessert later, then so be it. Have it your way."

She held up the necklace. "I like this necklace. What do you say?" She held it up against her neck. "After all, gotta look the part when the woman I love is so much younger than me."

Liz smirked and tilted her head. "You love me? Were you going to tell me that or make me guess?"

Marisa moved in and touched her finger along Liz's lips. Liz closed her eyes and leaned into the touch. "Thought you would have figured that out by now. I love you, Elizabeth Fletcher." She dropped the necklace back onto the top of Liz's dresser.

"I love you, Marisa. So much." She touched her lips against Marisa's. "But you can't wear that necklace," Liz whispered.

"And why not?" Marisa pouted.

"Chad gave it to me," Liz replied.

Marisa made a face and Liz nodded. She stepped forward to Marisa and pulled her into her arms. "Who needs jewelry? Or clothes, for that matter?" Liz asked.

She kissed Marisa hard, then pushed her back against the wall, nearly knocking Marisa's head against it. They kissed in a feverish and impassioned embrace. Marisa grabbed onto Liz's leg and wrapped it around hers, Liz's skirt inching up higher as Marisa pressed her hand on the inside of Liz's thigh, running her fingers up and under her panties. The warmth of Liz's sex touched Marisa's skin, and she flicked her tongue into Liz's waiting mouth.

"I want you," Marisa moaned.

Liz parted from the kiss, a sexy grin on her lips as she grabbed Marisa's hand and pulled her toward the bed. Marisa smiled. What was one reservation, anyway? Liz pressed her hand against Marisa's chest, knocking her back onto the bed. Marisa watched her as Liz straddled her legs, then moved down to kiss her. Marisa wrapped her hands around Liz's body, feeling around for the zipper on her back. As they kissed with a hunger that ignited the flames inside of them, the doorbell rang.

Liz groaned, breaking from the kiss. Marisa's mouth hung open. Talk about a buzzkill. She was left desperately hanging for the thrill that had been interrupted.

"You go ahead and look for a necklace. Any other one will do." Liz winked. "I'll get rid of whoever's at the door and we should just about make our reservations."

Marisa groaned as Liz reached for her hand and pulled her up. "Get rid of them and we could resume where we left off." Her eyes popped up and Liz laughed.

"You and I know it's hard to get into this restaurant. So, we should make it. But there's always dessert." She winked and then turned away.

Liz had this way about her that told Marisa everything would be all right. Marisa couldn't get rid of the images playing in her mind of Liz on top of her. They were, enough, for now. She just hoped she could make it to dessert.

With Liz gone, Marisa went back to the jewelry box, replaced the necklace that she wouldn't wear, and then grabbed another. She looked at her reflection and shifted her head from one side to the other, then back again. She liked it. She kept it in her hand and left her room, heading down to the foyer, where she could only make out soft voices.

"What about this one, babe?" she asked, entering the foyer.

Liz turned toward her, and her mouth dropped. Marisa glanced at the door to find a man standing there. His gaze darted between the two women. Liz uttered, "Marisa, this is Chad. Chad, Marisa."

Marisa felt all the blood drain from her face. She never meant to be introduced to Chad, let alone when they were moments ago in the throes of passion. She opened her mouth, but no words came out.

"I should go," Marisa said.

"No. I don't want you to." Liz reached out and touched Marisa's arm. Marisa caught the way Chad's eyes darted to her arm, and she felt uncomfortable.

"I'll go," he said, turning on his heel and rushing from the house. He got into his car and tore away from the house, the squealing of tires following after him. Liz looked at Marisa and shrugged, but all Marisa could do was gawk at her. Was this really something Liz was ready to work through?

THE TIME SLOWLY TICKED BY AS MARISA LOOKED OVER AT LIZ. They had been sitting in the living room for what felt like hours as she waited for Liz to say something. Anything. They had shared a few awkward glances and that was all. Marisa fidgeted in her chair.

"Listen, Liz. I don't want this to get any weirder. Maybe I

should just go, and you should run after him. I think you guys have some serious things that you need to hash out."

"It's not weird," Liz argued, shooting her a glance.

Marisa laughed and looked away from her, then down to her watch. "We've been sitting here for fifteen minutes with no more than two looks between us. It feels sort of weird. I'm not gonna lie."

Liz rubbed her face and made a guttural groan. "I'm sorry. I don't want things to be weird or awkward or anything like that. I wanted tonight to just be about us. I had no idea he was back in Chicago, and I certainly didn't expect him to pop in like that."

Marisa tilted her head. "When's the last time you talked?"

"Two weeks ago? Something like that. Guess I lost track of time. Once I set my heart on you, nothing else mattered."

Marisa quirked up her lips in a smile. She blushed and looked down at her clasped her hands. Liz knew exactly what to say at that moment. Marisa got up and went over to the couch to sit next to her. She reached out and held Liz's hand in hers. She traced her finger down her fingers and Liz smiled and cast a glance her way.

"Whether I stay or leave, it doesn't change that I'm here for the long haul, Liz. I've gotten past any insecurities about us being in a relationship. You are the one I want, and I will wait for you to get your baggage behind you. You have to know that."

"My baggage is behind me," Liz whispered, moving in.

Marisa didn't object to the kiss, but she kept it short and touched her fingers to Liz's puckered lips.

"Your baggage isn't truly behind you until you tell Chad that it's over."

Liz smirked. "I think he got that message when you came down the stairs looking like that."

She traced her finger under Marisa's chin and Marisa closed her eyes to her touch. How had things gotten to the point that they felt their chemistry finally coming alive?

Marisa opened her eyes and smiled. "You are the one woman who keeps me guessing and I love that. I love you." She gave a simple peck on Liz's lips, then stood up. "But, serious question coming your way. Are you ready for it?"

She tossed a look over her shoulder at Liz, who looked like a little kid huddled in the corner of her couch. She shrugged, which made Marisa turn to face Liz. "I don't know if I should ask it, then. I need you to be prepared to be honest."

"I'll be honest, Marisa. You don't have to worry about that. I'm not about to be anything but honest with you. You can trust me."

"I'm glad to hear that," Marisa said, kneeling down in front of Liz. "But there comes a moment where some answers might be difficult to come by."

"Such as?" Liz asked, leaning forward, her breath on Marisa's hands as Marisa rested her elbows on her knees.

"When you saw Chad this evening, did you have feelings?"

"Feelings? As in?" Liz scrunched up her face, a look of agony in her eyes.

"Feelings. You know, like maybe you were second-guessing your decisions. Like maybe you were fearing that what you felt for Chad was more than you were letting on?"

"Are you serious?" Liz asked, leaning back in her seat.

Marisa kept her gaze locked on Liz's. Liz shook her head. "No. Never. If anything, when I saw him, it made me realize that everything I'm feeling with you is true and real. It made me realize that my feelings for him were never genuine."

Marisa smiled, her heart warming up to those words. "I needed to hear that."

Marisa pulled herself up and sat next to Liz, pulling her in her arms. She kissed the top of her head and just held her. Liz helped Marisa to feel young again, a feeling that had long been forgotten and was everything Marisa wanted to get back to. How could she have ever turned away from that?

"Maybe we can get into our reservation just a little later," Liz whispered.

Marisa turned her head to see Liz's wide grin. "I just want to sit here with you," she replied.

She snaked her hand around Liz's and pulled her to her. They would have forever to spend going out as a couple. As long as they wanted one another, they would be there for each other. They parted from the kiss and Liz rested in the crook of Marisa's arm as Marisa held her closer. No matter what Liz needed from her, she would give it. Whatever it was, she was there to be her protector, and she was ready for whatever that entailed.

CHAPTER TWENTY

Liz

L iz's phone rang as she sat in the parking lot of the corner diner. She checked the clock on her dashboard. She had been watching for Chad for the past fifteen minutes and now wondered if maybe he had stood her up. He had seemed a bit hopeful on the phone when she called him earlier about meeting so they could talk. Yet, she still hadn't seen his red Camaro pull into the parking lot; maybe he had backed out.

She grabbed her phone, not recognizing the phone number. "Hello?"

"Hello, is this Elizabeth Fletcher?" the man on the phone asked.

"Yes, this is she."

"Hi, the name is Braxton Shaw. I got your name from your mother."

Liz frowned. "Okay…"

"The reason I'm calling is I am opening a pediatric clinic in Indianapolis. It's all in the preliminary stages, but I'll be looking for two to three nurses to help manage it, along with me, of course. Your name comes highly recommended."

Liz laughed. "By my mother? Is this a joke?"

He snickered on the other end of the line. "I can assure you, it's no joke. I've made a few calls as well, and can assure you that I'm not just taking your mother's word on this matter. I'm looking forward to building an empire here. You can do an Internet search for my name, and you'll see I'm not some sort of stalker."

Liz put the call on her speakerphone and pulled up a search engine. She entered his name and a picture came up, along with various charities he had worked with.

"From the silence, I assume you're looking at my picture right now."

She turned her attention back to the call. "So, you're interested in me. What now?"

"Well, that's up to you, really. But in the next few months, I'll be starting the hiring process. The building will be up and running in six months. If all goes well, that is. I would like to know if you would be interested if I were to call you back in three months."

Liz spotted Chad's car turning into the parking lot. She opened her door and stepped out of the car. "Give me a call. I just might be intrigued."

"I'm glad to hear that. You'll be hearing from me. Goodbye, Ms. Fletcher."

"Bye."

She disconnected the call and slipped her phone into her purse. Exactly what she needed—a job. Yet, she hesitated to take it. What would that mean for her relationship with Marisa? Would she be willing to uproot her own life for Liz?

She had to push that worry out of her mind as she entered the diner. Chad was in the corner booth, and she nodded her greeting to the waitress at the counter, then head over to where he sat. He looked up but didn't acknowledge her by standing up.

"Good afternoon," she said.

"Hey!" He closed the menu he had been looking at and smiled, but it appeared forced. "Let's order and then you can tell me why you brought me here."

His words were tense, and he didn't even look in her direction. It wasn't going to be an easy conversation to get through, but she was more ready than ever to make sure it happened.

They placed their orders and, once the waitress had left, Liz looked across the table. "Will you please at least look at me?" she asked.

He slowly looked up, but his eyes were dark. It wasn't the typical Chad that she was used to seeing. He appeared reclusive and quiet, like maybe he had been crying. But Chad didn't cry, and even if he had, Liz didn't care. He had been unfaithful.

"I won't take long. I just felt our relationship deserved to have some closure, if you will."

He clapped his hands in front of him. "If that's what you want to call it. Go right ahead."

"Chad," Liz started, "you don't need to be a jerk about this.

I mean, come on. If you're being honest, you know that we would never have made it. Be honest with yourself if you don't want to be honest with me."

He dropped his gaze to his hands, and she saw she was breaking him down. "Exactly! So, it is what it is. This is as good for you as it is for me. Because I'll tell you right here and now, Chad. I don't buy for one minute that you left your phone at a meeting. I heard you. The shower was running, and you called her babe. So, don't go giving me that."

He looked up, his eyes wide. "So, that's when you thought you would go out and have your own little rendezvous? 'Serves him right' sort of thing?"

Liz huffed, wanting to break into laughter, but it wasn't the place or time. "I didn't get with Marisa for revenge. That just happened."

"A woman." He shook his head. "And I thought I knew you."

"You thought you knew me? I thought I knew you. I thought you'd never cheat on me. But surprise, I was wrong. I didn't go out looking for Marisa. It did really just happen. But I was missing something. Marisa filled that void."

Again, his eyes dropped. Liz fought the urge to reach out to take his hand. There was no point in trying to show him compassion; it could lead to the wrong idea. She waited for him to look back up, but his eyes rested on the table.

"I never wanted to hurt you. And I want to believe you never meant to hurt me."

He looked up and shook his head. "Never! It, it, well, it just happened."

Liz nodded, smiling, knowing how that could happen. "If we

were meant to be, then it wouldn't have just happened. Not for either of us. And that's the truth."

He sighed and looked away from her. "When you're right, you're right."

He chuckled and even grinned, and Liz felt relief overwhelm her.

"I knew something was up," he said. "You rarely took my calls and then I got a call that blew things out of the water."

Liz frowned as he reached into his pocket and pulled out a ring box. He opened it up and pushed the ring toward Liz. "A friend of mine owns a pawn shop and called me when this beauty showed up."

"How did he know?" Liz asked.

"The inscription." He pulled the ring out of the box and turned it over. "I had told him when I got the ring but I never in a million years thought you would pawn it. I mean, that's not very classy. Not the woman I grew to know and love."

Liz's cheeks burned with embarrassment. "I didn't," she said. "I lost it and I called to tell you but then the woman answered. That was the turning point in our relationship—at least, in my opinion."

"Wow." He shook his head. "Guess it's a good thing it showed up in the right place, or else who knows if we would have ever found out what happened to it."

The waitress returned with their food, placing it in front of them.

"Thank you," Liz mumbled.

When the waitress left, she looked back at Chad. "I'm sorry things didn't work out, Chad. I really am."

"Neither of us was perfect. It happens. I wish you happiness,

Liz." He reached out and touched her hand. A smile crossed her lips.

"I wish you the same, Chad."

With those words, one path ended. Liz was ready for the full realization of everything she could have with Marisa, and she looked forward to that journey.

LIZ STEPPED INTO THE HOSPITAL AND SPOTTED HANNA HEADING to the front desk. She gave a wave when she saw Liz, but her eyes lacked their usual shine. Liz forced a smile. "Hey there. How are you?" she asked.

"I'm good. You?" Hanna fidgeted from one foot to the other. "I'm sorry about how things went."

"Don't be," Liz said. "Could be for the best." She thought of the call she had earlier and forced a smile. "Trust me, I'm not upset about it."

Hanna sighed. "Good. I didn't know if I should call you. I didn't want you to be mad at me or something."

"It's not your fault," Liz replied. "Don't worry about it."

"Okay." Hanna nodded. "Hope you're not needing to be seen today or anything."

Liz shook her head. "Came to see Marisa. But we definitely need to catch up soon. I have a ton to tell you."

Hanna smiled wider. "Sounds good. Take care." She pulled Liz into a hug before she went to call her patient.

Liz watched her as she grabbed the patient, a feeling of irritation coursing through her veins. No matter what she said to Hanna, she did feel upset that she had lost that job. She just had to believe that something better was out there. She turned and headed to the elevator. Once the doors closed on her, her phone rang. She took it out of her bag and noted the lack of bars at the top right corner of the phone.

"Hello?" she quickly answered.

"H…Li…how…"

Then, silence.

"Hello? Can you hear me?"

"Liz…" Then silence.

"Hold on. I'm on the elevator," Liz yelled into the phone. She looked up at the numbers on the elevator, then finally reached her floor. When the doors opened, she rushed out of the elevator. "Hello?"

"Liz? Can you hear me?"

"I can hear you."

"Good. This is Victoria, Donovan's mother."

The blood rushed from Liz's face as she fell back against the wall. Beads of sweat piled up on her forehead. It felt like an eternity since she had last spoken to her. Why was Victoria contacting her now?

"Hey, Victoria." She braced herself for the worst. "I'm surprised to hear from you."

"Well, it took a while before I could get someone to give me your number. I finally got ahold of Marisa today at the hospital and she was eager to give me your number. How are you?"

"I, I'm fine," Liz stuttered. "But, more importantly, how's Donovan?"

"Well, that's the reason I'm calling."

Liz held her breath. Was that nerves that she heard coming

from Victoria? She wanted to start crying already, but she had to be strong for Donovan's mother.

"Yeah?" she asked.

"Donovan and I went to Tennessee for his treatment, as I'm sure you heard. There's a specialist here that the staff at Capmed thought could work well with Donovan. Well, it turns out they were right."

Liz released the breath she was holding. "They were?" she asked.

"Yep. Treatment is going well and they're even talking about him being able to go home soon and continuing his care on an outpatient basis. His leukemia is in remission. You were the first one he wanted to call. And he's here right now, anxious to talk to you."

"I'm so happy." Liz covered her face, tears—happy ones, this time—threatening to fall.

"Liz?" Donovan came onto the phone, and everything she had feared about his condition was washed away with the tears that streamed down her cheeks.

"Donovan! I'm so happy to hear from you. Not a day has gone by that I haven't thought about you. You and your mom. How are you?"

She wanted to talk to him about so many things, but just hearing his voice was more than enough. She had feared that she would never find out how he was doing. Now that she had their number, she wouldn't have to worry about that anymore.

Unfortunately, they couldn't stay on the phone long, as Donovan had therapy he had to get to, but even the fifteen minutes they had put Liz in a better place.

"Call me again soon," she said to Veronica as Donovan handed the phone back to her.

"I will. But thank you for everything."

"It's been my pleasure."

Liz disconnected the call, wiping away the rest of her tears. She put her phone away and headed toward the lab. Samantha sat at the front desk and looked up the moment Liz walked into the lobby. She gave a weak smile.

"Hi," Liz said. "Is Marisa back there?"

Samantha nodded. "Head on back."

Liz smiled and went through the door. Marisa looked up and got up from her desk. "Well, to what do I owe this pleasure?" she asked.

"Just got off the phone with Victoria," Liz replied. "You gave her my number?"

"I knew you'd want to take that call." She shrugged. "Great news, wasn't it?"

"The best." Liz wrapped her arm around Marisa and pulled her to her. They kissed, and when Marisa pulled back, Liz brushed a strand of hair behind Marisa's ear. "I love you so much!"

"I love you more," Marisa whispered.

"I saw Chad today, and I have officially put that all behind me. We've realized that our relationship would have never worked. You, on the other hand, were always meant to be my destiny."

"Oh, is that so?" A sexy grin rested on Marisa's lips.

Liz bit her lower lip and nodded. She looked over to the door and then back to Marisa. "What time is your next appointment?"

"Twenty minutes," Marisa quietly answered.

"Then we'd best hurry," Liz replied. She kissed Marisa, pressing her back up against the desk. The heat had already gone straight to her inner thighs, and she didn't even care if someone walked in on them. Why hold back when she had everything she needed right there?

EPILOGUE

Marisa

Three Months Later

Would you ever be willing to move to Indianapolis? Those words had played through Marisa's mind a couple hundred times since Liz had brought up the fact that she had been offered an opportunity to work in Indiana.

It had been three months, and Liz had received a few offers of employment, but they didn't seem a good match for her. She had continued to do volunteer work at the hospital, but even Marisa knew that Liz didn't like being there when she wasn't getting paid for it. Marisa hated seeing the struggle in Liz's eyes. And she would never hold Liz back from getting something she truly wanted out of life. So, yes, that question went through Marisa's mind in a repeated loop.

If Indianapolis were what Liz wanted, then Marisa would graciously follow her. She would follow her to the ends of the earth if that's what Liz wanted. Although, there was something in Marisa's mind that told her she needed to see if there was another option for Liz.

She stepped out of the elevator and, instead of stopping at the desk, went straight for Trace Reece's office. She knew if anyone could help her out, it'd be him. Luckily, he was there. He looked up when she knocked and got up from his desk. "Marisa. This is a surprise."

"This won't take long." Marisa released a shaky breath. "You know how hard Liz works for you. She comes in and volunteers when needed. She's a grade A worker, but she should be paid for her job. And I like to believe that you know this."

Trace itched his beard and tilted his head. "I also know the hospital has no openings."

"Then make one," she exclaimed. She stepped back. "I'm sorry. I know that it's not that easy to just make a job when there isn't one, but I hate seeing her struggling to find a job. If she doesn't get one, she's headed to Indiana, and you'll use your best volunteer."

He quirked up an eyebrow, then sat back down in his seat. "She is a great nurse. I know this."

"The best," Marisa said. He looked up and nodded. "She's caring and dedicated, and you do not want to lose her."

"And she obviously has a great advocate in you."

Marisa shrugged. "Just trying to do what's right. It would be a shame to lose her. Right?"

Trace's silence killed her, but after a while he nodded his head. "I'll tell you what. I'm with you on this one. I'm sure there's enough in the budget for one more nurse. We haven't hired on this floor in a while. So, have her come see me tomorrow."

Marisa clapped her hands together. "Really?"

He nodded.

"Thank you so much." She shook his hand and he gave her a bright smile.

As she left the office, she was surprised that things had come together like they had and in such a short amount of time. She hurried out of the hospital, but once she got back to her car, she worried. What if Liz didn't want to stay here? What if she would rather take the gig in Indianapolis? It was something she had to consider, at least. This wasn't her call. It was solely Liz's.

The whole way to her house, she worried about butting in when perhaps she shouldn't have. "Stop fretting," she finally told herself. "If she doesn't want it, then that's fine. At least you tried."

She turned into Liz's driveway and practiced exactly how she would begin the conversation. She knocked on the door and waited for Liz to answer. When she didn't come to the door, Marisa tried ringing the doorbell. Again, nothing. She tried the door, and it opened right away. She peeked her head through the door, feeling strange just barging in.

"Liz?" she called out.

"In the dining room," Liz responded.

Marisa walked down the hallway and rounded the corner. Liz stood next to a table that was adorned with candles and flowers. Marisa's jaw dropped.

"What's this?" Marisa asked.

"Can't I do something nice for you?" Liz replied, grinning.

"I thought we were going out?"

Marisa moved closer to Liz, who pulled her in for a kiss. Marisa responded enthusiastically, but the nagging urge to tell Liz what Marisa had done on her behalf kept running through her head. She parted from the kiss.

"I'm sorry, I can't do this," she started.

Liz frowned. "You can't do what?"

"This romantic evening without telling you what's happened."

Liz rested against a chair. "Do I need to sit?" she asked.

Marisa shook her head. "It's nothing like that. You see, I just wanted to help. I wanted you to have options and so I went to Trace Reece and talked to him about a job on the children's floor."

"You did that for me?"

Marisa nodded. "I wanted to see if there was anything he thought he could do. But now that I think about it, I realize how foolish that was. I mean, you might want to go to Indy, and I'm not going to get in your way, and I think I should have allowed you to make up your mind."

Liz looked away, her eyes going to the table. Marisa followed her gaze, but then Liz turned to look at her. There were tears in her eyes and a smile on her lips. "Marisa, this wasn't how I wanted this evening to go. I had everything planned out. From dinner and romance to even dancing later."

Marisa smiled. "And I had my own plans to pan out. But we've never been the traditional couple and plans are meant to be broken, right?"

Liz smirked and nodded. "Let me tell you what I had planned. You see, I put this together so I could tell you that really the only thing I could possibly want out of life was you. I don't need a lavish job or a corner office or anything like that. What I need is to know that we're together and we're happy. So, two hours ago, I called Braxton Shaw and turned the job down. Because what I really want is you. That's all. And even if I don't get back into Capmed, I know that you and I will be together."

Marisa grinned. "Well, you're to report in tomorrow."

Liz shook her head. "You are amazing. How did I get so lucky?"

Liz moved in and kissed her. Marisa's heart raced, and she felt like she was the lucky one. No doubts about that.

"There's one more thing." Liz reached over to the table and pulled a napkin up. Beneath the napkin was a ring box. Marisa's jaw dropped as Liz turned to her. She knelt down on her knee and stared up at Marisa. "I know what I want. Please marry me. I want to spend the rest of this crazy life with you and only you."

Marisa felt tears crowding her eyes. She knelt down in front of Liz. "There's just one problem." She slipped her hand into her pocket and pulled out a box. She opened it up and looked up at Liz. "I was going to ask you."

Liz began to laugh, and they both looked down at the ring that was in the other box. They met each other's gaze and Marisa pulled Liz into her arms. They both knew the answer. Saying it could wait. Together forever. It was the greatest feeling in the world, and they would have every day to spend together proving that love was always worth the fight.

MT CASSEN BOOKS

Available In Paperback, Ebook, And Audio Formats. Click Here:
https://mybook.to/MELODYINHERHEART

Available In Paperback, Ebook, And Audio Formats. Click Here:
https://mybook.to/FIGHTINGHERTOUCH

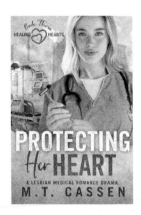

Available In Paperback, Ebook, And Audio Formats. Click Here:
https://mybook.to/PROTECTINGHERHEART

Available In Paperback, Ebook, And Audio Formats. Click Here:
https://mybook.to/TOOLITTLETOOLATE

YOU CAN HELP OTHERS!

A big thank you for trusting my book with your time, attention, and support. Here are three points to remember about reader comments (aka book reviews):

1. I read all reader comments so I can fix any errors and make my next book even better. "***Get busy polishing or get busy rusting***," is my motto as a writer. I believe that good books are brought forth consistently when an author's persistence is enabled by the generous expressions of reader intent as seen in reviews and purchases.
2. Most readers read the reviews to help guide their purchases. I don't buy anything before looking at the reviews. Your reviews help readers.
3. Now, you're all ready to drop a comment, but analysis paralysis gets the better of you. You might

think: *What would I even write about? Who's going to read my review, anyway?*

Well, for starters, I will read your reviews. Also, so will many readers. So, please snap out of your analysis paralysis. To help you get started, I have added here some questions on which other readers would want your opinions:

- What did you think of Marisa? What did you like or not like about her?
- What did you think of Liz? What would you do if you were in her shoes?
- What would you like to communicate to other readers (including Aunt Susie) who may be interested in this book?

Think of these questions as kick-starters for your review.

Please drop your honest opinions here:
https://www.amazon.com/review/create-review?
ASIN=B0B5B6RVWM
or click or scan the QR code below;

That would make my day! Thank you!
Please grab a free book below:

https://BookHip.com/LJDAWWT
Or click or scan the QR code below:

Happy Reading,

Morgan

P.S: Thanks, www.kindlepreneur.com, for the QR code generator, and www.booklinker.com for the universal links.

ABOUT THE AUTHOR

Morgan Cassen
WITH ROXIE

Morgan Cassen writes Lesbian Romance. Her mission is to make the world safer for sapphic stories to be told. Yes, she knows that there are millions of romance writers and billions of romance novels. So, why would she even think of adding to the pile? Well, Morgan has seen enough to know that the truly interesting stories are not what happen between human beings. That gig can seem pretty tame. At least compared to its older, tempestuous sister. Let's bring out Ms. Inner Conflict, the queen of all drama in the human world -- the ruler of the emotional map. Yes, the conflict between everything you've worked for and everything you want. You never imagined that all your hard work would put you so far away from everything you wanted. Also, how about the conflict between the past and the future? Being true to the past would require you to keep the future so far away in the future. But, how long can you postpone the future? What if your whole framing of the past can't stand the scrutiny of thoughtful analysis today even as you resolutely push the future away? Huh, what do you do with that kind of conflict? The conflict between human beings can look so tame compared to the real thing: conflict between you and you. You are the hero and villain at the same time, but the problem is that the villain thinks she is the hero, while the hero is all caught up in doubt. Which you will you choose? No, nobody else will make that choice for you. You get to make that choice, and your comforting, trusty friend--procrastination--can't seem to do the trick this time. The time has come for you to choose. See, inner conflict is where it's at. Inner conflict is what Morgan writes about in her books. Please join her as she writes the stories of breakup and love that tug at heartstrings.

Morgan is indebted to Sarah Wu (copyeditor) and Dr. Peter Palmieri and Nurse Karen Stockdale (medical advisors) for their extraordinary work and diligence. This book is so much better because of their efforts.

Stalk the author using the link below:

www.mtcassen.com

ABOUT PETER PALMIERI
(MEDICAL ADVISOR)

Peter Palmieri, M.D., M.B.A. is a licensed physician with over 20 years of practice experience in Chicago, Dallas, Houston, and the Rio Grande Valley in Texas. He received his B.A. from the University of California San Diego, with a double major in Animal Physiology and Psychology. He earned his medical degree from Loyola University Stritch School of Medicine and a Healthcare M.B.A. from The George Washington University. He is a regular contributor of original articles to a variety of health and wellness blogs.

ABOUT KAREN STOCKDALE
(MEDICAL ADVISOR)

Karen Stockdale, MBA, BSN, RN is an experienced nurse in the fields of cardiology and medical/surgical nursing. She has also worked as a nurse manager, hospital quality and safety administrator, and quality consultant. She obtained her ASN-RN in 2003 and her BSN in 2012 from Southwest Baptist University. Karen completed an MBA in Healthcare Management in 2017. She currently writes for several healthcare and tech blogs and whitepapers, as well as developing continuing education courses for nurses.

Karen's websites are:
https://www.linkedin.com/in/karen-stockdale-5aab2584/
and
http://writemedical.net/

ABOUT SARAH WU
(COPYEDITOR)

Sarah was born and raised in the concrete jungle of NYC. She loves traveling, exploring different foods, and giving the occasional tree a big hug. When Sarah isn't polishing up manuscripts, she enjoys spending time with loved ones and lovingly but firmly heckling them to decrease their plastic consumption.

Printed in Great Britain
by Amazon